TINY WORLDS

VOLUME TWO

J. CURTIS

For new stories, visit TinyWorlds.substack.com

Tiny Worlds | Volume Two

Cover design by Shane Bzdok
Photography by J. Curtis

———

The Zeno Paradox edited by S.E. Reid

Two Palms Motel written with Jason Thompson

———

First Edition 2025
Paperback ISBN 979-8-9924626-2-3
Ebook ISBN 979-8-9924626-6-1

———

R-3

CONTENTS

For my cheering squad: G, J, I

INTRODUCTION

This is my eighth—or maybe tenth—draft of this introduction. I scrapped what came before and started over. Too many edits, too many hours spent pushing pixels around trying to say things I'm not sure I'm qualified to say. Think of it as a mercy killing.

The one piece I'll keep, mostly intact, from those previous drafts is this: *ideas change us*. You, me, everyone. Not the words themselves but something unwritten that leaves a trace.

If we're honest, they don't even have to be shiny new ideas, really. It can be last season's idea, or an idea found at the discount store, or tucked between the pages of a dusty tome you found at a secondhand bookstore.

The point here is that an idea you happened upon— from wherever—changed you in some way. It shifted your thinking ever so slightly.

And if we go just a bit further, the writer of that idea probably has no way of knowing they did that. And never will. I'd like to have a fancy name for this interaction, like intellectual osmosis, but I think *serendipity* pretty much fits the bill.

You see, writing—being what it is—is a mostly solo job. It's a one-person tennis match with no scorekeeper. And after some months or years, that thing you wrote is out there, holding this idea without your interaction. Writers don't get to choose their audience or stand over their shoulder and point out some turn of phrase they find interesting. We don't get to underline passages for our readers.

So, reading and absorbing those words becomes a solo act, too.

But sometimes, with far less precision than we might hope for, an idea lands in a fertile pasture. And it blooms if the conditions are right.

Sometimes quickly—think of any bestseller that caught fire. Or among the shelf of books at a vacation rental, forgotten and overlooked, until it's plucked to sit poolside with you and be discovered later. But that act—the idea growing and becoming a new window to view life—is really the point, not the timing of it.

Changing perceptions with only a handful of words is the thing writers aspire to. It's what I've been chasing in every story in this collection

This is my second book, and it lands around my 51st birthday. That wasn't really planned, but it feels right. Another quiet gift to myself. No champagne, no party. Just a way of saying: I'm still doing the work. Still showing up. Still trying to figure these things out. Proof that whatever this is —a need to explore ideas, to wonder—still has me chasing what stories can do.

And maybe that's the point.

We're not just telling stories. We're trying to send something into the world that might matter, might endure—even if the ideas within are something we don't fully understand.

Writing won't save lives. It won't stop storms or cure disease.

But it can still reach something quiet and human—the part of us that shifts slowly, that listens differently after a good story, that starts to ask better questions.

Not wholly because of what we wrote—but because of what you carry with you.

If one of these stories lingers in your mind, if it tugs at you days later in the middle of something else, I hope you'll let it.

And if you feel like it, drop me a line and say so. No rush.

J. Curtis
June 2025

SKETCHBOOK

These are *like a pencil sketch with words*; loose, unrefined and not wholly a thing. But I like them and think there's something here you might like, too.

READING IN THE NUDE

The two men sat in their usual corner of the retirement home's common room. A late afternoon sun cast long stripes across the worn carpet.

Most of the residents had retired to their rooms for naps, leaving the space still and quiet. But these two lingered, as they always did, spinning tales and sharing philosophies.

The first man, dressed in a silk robe, crossed one leg over the other and sipped his tea. "I only write when I'm dressed for it. Silk for thrillers—smooth and slippery, like the plot twists. You need to feel like the story's seeping through you, right?"

The second man, draped in a tweed jacket over his worn pajamas, nodded thoughtfully. "Same here. But for mysteries, it's tweed all the way. Makes me feel like I'm out solving the case, like every word I type could crack it wide open."

"And the pipe?" the first man teased, gesturing to the unlit burled pipe sitting on the table beside his friend.

"Essential," the second man replied, tapping it lightly. "Even if I can't smoke it anymore, it gets me in the zone."

They both chuckled, but the second man's smile turned up, a delicious thought forming.

"But when I read…" he said in a secretive whisper, "it's a whole other story. I strip down—nothing but me and the book. That's how the words truly get in, unfiltered."

The first man leaned back, his silk robe shifting with the motion. "Same here. Writing needs the costume, the illusion. Reading, though? That's where you let everything fall away."

The door creaked open, and Nurse Clara entered with her usual cheery efficiency. "Everything alright in here, gentlemen?" she asked, glancing at the thermostat as she passed.

"Perfectly fine," said the first man with a wry grin. "But if you're adjusting that thing, make it warmer. My creativity thrives at seventy-five."

"More like seventy-eight," the second man muttered, wrapping his tweed jacket tighter.

Clara smirked as she fiddled with the dial. "Just keeping it comfortable for everyone. And don't worry, I'll be back with your meds soon."

As she left, the two men shared a conspiratorial glance. "She thinks we're crazy," said the first man, chuckling.

"Maybe we are," replied the second, shrugging. "Who else sits here debating costumes like they're knights preparing for battle?"

"Knights," mused the first man. "Good call. For fantasy, I wear a full wizard's robe. Velvet, stars, the works."

"Velvet?" the second man said, eyebrows raised. "Too heavy. I'm more of an adventurer—leather vest, boots, a satchel over my shoulder."

"And for horror?" the first man asked.

"Oh, horror's simple," said the second man with a grin.

"A tattered bathrobe, maybe with a hood. Enough to feel the dread but not scare the staff."

"For me, it's all trench coat, my collar turned up," the first man replied. "Shadows do the rest."

They lapsed into a comfortable silence, the room warm with camaraderie and the faint hum of the heater. After a while, the second man broke the quiet. "You ever think about the people reading our work? What they're wearing, I mean?"

The first man tilted his head, considering. "What about the people reading *this*?"

"Hmm," the second man said, leaning forward. His expression turned serious, almost haunted, as his gaze drifted not to the window, nor the door Clara had passed through, but somewhere else—past the edges of the room.

The first man followed his line of sight. His brow furrowed as his gaze scanned the space around him, pausing as if seeing something just out of reach.

"Hmm," he murmured. "Yes. I suppose they're out there, aren't they? Watching. Reading."

The second man sat back in his chair, but his eyes didn't waver. Now they roamed higher, drifting over what seemed to be nothing but empty air. And yet, with each subtle twist of his head, his eyes closed in, searching.

Slowly, both men stopped moving. With narrowed eyes they focused just beyond the page. They looked to the header and saw the title:

READING IN THE NUDE

Finally, the second man locked on something far beyond the room. "Do you see them?" he asked.

The first man nodded slowly. "Oh, I see them." His lips curled into a sly smile. He sat up straighter, adjusting his robe. "They're reading these words *right now*."

There was a long silence between them as their focus deepened, their eyes locked, just beyond the veil.

The second man finally spoke, his voice a low rasp, "You." He pointed, a slow, deliberate gesture. "Yeah, *you*. Sitting there, reading this story. How are you dressed?"

The first man leaned forward, his silk robe pooling around him like a ripple. "Are you in your coziest sweater, maybe curled up with a mug of tea? Wrapped in a blanket like a proper mystery reader?"

"Or maybe something dramatic?" the second man added, his grin sharp now. "A trench coat, a fedora for noir. A wizard's robe for fantasy. Or—" he paused, his tone growing daring, as his eyes sparkled—"maybe nothing at all? Sitting there, bare, letting the story touch you completely."

The first man raised an eyebrow, his chin dipping as though expecting a response only he could hear. "It matters, you know. How you approach it. How you show up. A story can only take you as far as you're willing to go."

The second man gave a knowing nod. "So? What's it going to be? Are you fully in it? Fully here? Or are you just *skimming*, pretending to be a part of this world while keeping your distance?"

The two men watched for a long moment, their eyes lingering—waiting. Not for each other, but for *you*, the reader.

Their voices softened, as if speaking directly to the reader now:

"Think about it," the first man said, a smirk in his tone.

"Because we are," the second said, adding a small chuckle. Then a wink.

The first laughed, boisterous and gravelly.

And then, just as suddenly, their eyes turned away after one last look—the thread pulled taut and quietly snipped.

Attention returned to the quiet room, the hum of the heater.

Somewhere beyond the room, beyond the ink and screen-glow, the question lingered.

Waiting for you to catch up.

———

Music to read by:
Cast Away - Alan Silvestri

AUNT STELLA

MY AUNT STELLA—GAWD, SHE WAS A CARD. ALWAYS THE LIFE of the party, with that grin and those awful teeth. I wouldn't say she lit up a room, but hell, did she make an entrance.

We all lived together for a short while in our little traveling circus, and it was then that I heard about her strange habits. They were the talk of everyone around.

She never talked, you know. Just stared at people for a long time. It freaked out every circus goer who came near. I guess that's why she was there. One time, she scared some kids so badly they shit themselves. Swear to it, saw it with my own beady eyes.

She was a rough-and-tumble woman who tried to push everyone around, including me and my siblings. During our swims, she'd roll in the mud, holding us down. Quite an awful thing, really, to be pulled under again and again.

You know, she had a thing for the strongman—with his bulging biceps and overly manicured mustache. He'd taunt her with his winks, throwing a scrap or two of affection now and then. He was a real tease. One night, that fella had one too many and stumbled into Aunt Stella on his way back to the caravans.

With a quick flick of her backside, Aunt Stella knocked him down into the water. We all watched, wanting to jump in and help, but she had her way with him right then and there. Serves him right, I suppose. It took a week for anyone to find even a shred of him.

The next day, Stella had her picture taken with some ugly woman in a bathing suit. Who wears an outfit like that for a portrait?

I mean, being an alligator is hard enough if nobody fucks with you.

BETH/VERONICA

A LONE SPOTLIGHT PINNED HER LIKE A SECRET TOO DELICIOUS to share, her curves carved out of smoke and shadow, her presence pulling audible gasps from the crowd. She stood there, the serpent of her performance winding itself around her body, bending and curling to trace every dip and swell. On that stage, she wasn't just the moon—she was a celestial tease, the Milky Way spilling over the edge, impossible to touch but begging you to try.

Her face was framed in suggestion, the faintest shimmer on her cheeks and lips as red as the devil's signature. No masks, no pretense, just the long, languid stretch of her neck, the dangerous angle of her legs slicing through the blue haze of light.

Beyond the glow, her audience were nothing more than hungry shapes—eyes glittering, mouths slack, shifting in their seats as their pulses found a rhythm she controlled. When the band played, their chords buzzed through her body like a low, intimate hum, setting her every move to a tempo of want. She had them, every last one of them, hooked and twitching on her line. A spilled drink here, a bitten lip there, the telltale sigh of someone losing control under her spell.

She moved like sin wrapped in satin, every flick of her hips a sly whisper, every stretch of her limbs a promise she'd never keep. They leaned forward, so desperate for more, and when she was ready to finish them off, she hit them where it hurt best—low, deep, and unrelenting. Her smile? A slow, wicked blade. Her glance? A hand sliding over their thighs, stopping just short of heaven. When she hit the final move, it sent shudders through their spines, starting below the belt and detonating somewhere between the heart and the head.

And she? She *felt* it, oh yes, tasted it on her tongue as their lust spilled out and flooded the air. Her skin gleamed like a satin sheet left rumpled after midnight, the freckles on her shoulders trembling in the light like secrets about to break loose. Her hair, tangled and damp, clung to her neck, a dark trap framing a vision of pale, irresistible decadence. Even she wasn't immune to the fever—womanhood coiled hot in her belly, rising like steam, making her drunk on the weight of all those eyes drinking her in. She was the garnish in their cocktail of longing, the citrus twist that made the bitter burn just right.

When the band reached its climax, so did she. Beth was gone, buried beneath the heat and hunger. She was *Veronica* now, her name rolling through their minds like the moans they'd try to stifle later. She wasn't just a woman; she was a possession they could never hold, a memory they'd take home like a stolen kiss.

They'd sit in their beds that night, their suits damp, their thoughts dirtier than their alibis. And when the sun rose, it would be Beth picking up groceries at the market. But when darkness fell again, and the lights dimmed, they'd come crawling back, their wallets open, their mouths dry, ready to lose themselves to Veronica once more.

———

Music to read by:
Red Arrow Inn - Mark Isham

LOVE POTIONS NO. 1-8

Egad... *Ruth*?

The Clovers—nice guys, but not very smart.

Boys, it's **Ruza**, roll your *r's* and let that *zed* have some bite.

Now that the internet is a thing and the statute of limitations on my story has lapsed, I can tell you this: I invented *Love Potion No. 9*. Yeah, that's right. And before you ask—no, it wasn't in some dingy little lab. I mean, I wasn't wearing a white coat—you have to picture something with a bit more flair, a lot more mess, and fewer safety protocols.

You see, love has always fascinated me. Maybe it's my gypsy roots—Romania, born and raised—where everything is a little more... magical. People everywhere are always looking for shortcuts to romance, a sprinkle of magic to get things moving. So, I thought, why not give them a little push? I set out to make a potion that could unlock hearts, stoke passions, or at least make people more willing to hold hands without breaking into a cold sweat.

But here's the thing—making a love potion isn't like baking cookies. It's more like trying to assemble a croquembouche on a houseboat while being chased by a lynx. A lot of improvisation, a lot of swearing, and mostly, a lot of mistakes.

Of course, if you know anything about gypsy culture, we don't exactly do paperwork. Recipes are passed down by word of mouth, and everyone adds their own twist—throw in a new location and the whole thing goes pear-shaped faster than you can say "nimble fingers nurture the noxious nightshade".

In Romania, where I'm from, you can find what you need with a bit of patience and a sharp knife. Eye of newt? Not hard if you only need a couple, but move to Philly— where the Puritans, literally, stomped the hell out of this place with their witch-hunting boots—and suddenly, you're between the hammer and the anvil. Newts are scarce, and let me tell you, mustard seed does not cut it in the magic department, no matter what the cookbooks say.

Let me get a cup of tea and I'll tell you the whole story...

BATCH NO. 1

Ah, my first attempt. Ambitious, to say the least. I was aiming for something rich and indulgent—a romantic treat, you know? I thought, "Who doesn't love dark chocolate?" So I whipped up some chocolate squares, tossed in a bit of guar extract (because, why not?), and waited for the magic to happen. Spoiler alert: it didn't. Turns out, too much guar extract doesn't lead to romance—it leads straight to the washroom. Yup, my would-be Casanovas were too busy running to fall in love. But hey, I licensed the recipe to Ex-Lax. Still cashing in on that one!

BATCH NO. 2

I went for something bold—garlic and paprika. The smell was divine! But instead of inspiring passion, it made everyone smell like a Sunday roast. The less said about this one, the better.

BATCH NO. 3

You'd think I'd learn after Batch #1, but no. I tried to tweak the formula, and somehow I managed to make it worse. If Batch #1 was a mild laxative, Batch #3 was… well, let's just say it was explosive. I don't know how, but I multiplied the effect by 100. Sorry, Hezekiah. And Tobar. And Bavol. Those poor guys. To this day, they still avoid anything I offer them that isn't clearly labeled.

BATCH NO. 4

Okay, so now I was determined. Less focus on digestion, more on love. This time I thought, "Why not try something calming?" So I added lavender. It's soothing, right? Helps you sleep, makes you relax—figured it would mellow everyone out, open them up to a little romance. Well, I didn't account for my dog, Chavula, getting into the mix. He lapped up a few drops when I wasn't looking and spent the next few hours licking himself like a maniac. Note: Chavula's fine now, and the hair's grown back.

BATCH NO. 5

Ah, the West Coast—where everyone was buzzing about a new plant. People were blending it into smoothies, baking it into brownies, and praising its many "health benefits." The bitterness was a challenge, though. After days of effort, I finally realized I was spending way too much time trying to make kale palatable. You wackos can keep my smoothie recipe!

BATCH NO. 6

North Carolina. Two months there, and I thought I'd hit the jackpot. This guy named Popcorn—yes, Popcorn—taught me how to make moonshine. Apparently, it's just whiskey without the patience, which I can get behind. Popcorn helped me brew some strong stuff—100% proof, no less. We had a blast, but a gypsy like me can't be hauling around all that distilling equipment. Popcorn still sends me a case now and again. I just use a little for a kick in my potions. Who knew a bit of moonshine could get people feeling real friendly?

BATCH NO. 7

O, Dumnezeule! Things were starting to get interesting now. By this point, my regulars were very cautious. They showed up in clothes that were easy to wash—smart. Now, here's a word you don't hear every day in a gypsy camp: vasodilation. The guys loved it, but the womenfolk? They were not impressed. Back to the cauldron.

BATCH NO. 8

This one had promise—or so I thought. I'd finally gotten my confidence back, and the usual test subjects were starting to trust me again. This time, I expanded the group to include the ladies from my book club. Everything seemed great during the day, but come nightfall, as they walked home through the forest, something... magical happened. Their skin started to glow. And not in that radiant, "you look amazing" way, but in a creepy, pale-witch kind of way. Their moaning and bellyaching on the walk home sure did raise eyebrows with the locals.

BATCH NO. 9

Un câştigat! Finally, after all those misfires, I struck gold. And no, I can't give away the details—trade secrets and all that—but let's just say it involves a fair amount of **[redacted]** and more than a hint of **[redacted]** for sweetness. This was the breakthrough I needed. The rest, as they say, is history.

Oh, and by the way, yes, I really do have a gold tooth. If you stop by the store, there's no kitchen sink involved. I've got bottles already made up.

If you're good-looking the first taste is free.

———

Music to read by:
Love Potion No. 9 by The Clovers

GOING HOME

Today is my birthday.

Today is also, as it was meant to be, my last day on Earth.

The cards and greetings that came via text were nice, but none of them had a clue what was really happening. They smiled, nodded, and mentioned plans for tomorrow.

But tomorrow? Tomorrow isn't even on the map.

I've been waiting for this day with a quiet thrill. It took years of planning—adjusting to this body, preparing the basement with tools most people would never understand. Diagrams, measurements, chemical reactions. I could almost feel the portal humming beneath my feet.

It was ready. I was ready.

Her kids were out of the house, and she was too. I washed the dishes, let the dog out one last time. Standing in the doorway, I glanced around the home she built. A beautiful place, no doubt. But a guest is a guest, and it was time for me to leave.

The old wooden steps creak beneath me, like they're bidding me farewell. I didn't feel heavy, though—this was a day of lightness, of anticipation. I couldn't help but smile.

Everything in place. No interruptions.

"Let's do this," I whispered, more to the universe than to myself.

Stepping to the edge of the portal, the energy buzzed around me, calling me, pulling me.

The drop isn't far—barely the length of my body—but this isn't about the fall. This is about the leap. Coming here was a mission—to witness, to learn. The return is a choice.

The air crackles with a low hum as I feel the last grip with these hands. My body is humming. My pulse races, not from fear, but from the sheer thrill of what's to come. I've been pretending for far too long.

5... 4...

Outside, I hear her car pulling up. The house is starting to shake. I'm sure she can feel it. Doesn't matter now.

3... 2...

The portal opens beneath me, glowing with cosmic energy, pulling me back to where I belong.

Footsteps above. Running.

1...

I let go.

Gravity disappears. I am not falling—I'm soaring. My body dissolves, light and energy unraveling as I leave behind the clumsy human form. The universe embraces me. I am free, expanding into something vast, infinite. The stars swirl around me, familiar, welcoming.

Home.

The weight of Earth fades, and the distance between me and the stars closes in a blink. My home world, vibrant and electric, rushes up to meet me. The colors, the energy—I can feel it all. I am no longer confined. I am myself again.

Today is my birthday.

JESUS TAKES A SABBATICAL

"Holy shit!" Jesus exclaims as the glass door closes behind him.

The office is in shambles.

Papers litter the floor, alarms blare, and employees cower under desks. A fire smolders somewhere, the scent of melted cubicle walls and plastic thick in the air. Phones ring incessantly. Any answered call is met with, "Good morning, can you hold?"

Gavreel—normally chill—rushes up. Months of unwashed hair twist in knots. A luggage store has opened and promptly gone out of business beneath her eyes.

"Is it really you? Are you back?" Gav asks, looking like she's seen a ghost.

"Yeah, it was just a holiday—"

Gavreel starts to cry.

"Email? Texts?"

Jesus digs into his satchel. "...My phone plan, hang on."

He hands Gav a baguette, then a fish, then more baguettes.

She drops them to the floor, where they shatter into a thousand more.

"Oh, Christ—" Gav mutters, knocking the phone from his hands. "We're overrun with prayers!"

"Okay, take a deep breath. Let's—"

She cuts him off. "The KKK is back. So are the Nazis!"

A Keurig explodes at the coffee bar.

"Oh, that's not so good. But I thought we—"

"Trust me, they're back. That fella said they were 'very fine people'!"

"Who cares what he said—"

"Guess who's running the country now?" Gavreel shouts.

Jesus rubs his temples, remembering the unfinished paperwork in his desk.

Gavreel stretches her neck, exhausted, blowing a matted clump of hair from her face.

Jesus licks his lips, parched. "But... my people—"

"Christians? Jesus! It's like they forgot everything while you were away."

He shifts, thinking.

Jesus suddenly regrets that extra week of silent meditation in Joshua Tree.

Gav grabs his shoulder, grounding him. "Even people from California are praying."

Another barrage of telephones. They just won't stop ringing.

"Fuuu..." Jesus looks around, taking a deep breath. "But what about..."

"Nope. The Pope's dodging our calls."

His sandals suddenly feel tight, uncomfortable. He wonders if he bought the wrong size.

The robe, too, feels a bit hot for the office. He freezes, cocking his head to one side, weighing his next question.

"Does my dad know?"
Gavreel meets his eyes, nodding slightly.
Jesus winced.

INFINITE & IMPROBABLE SHAPES

Her arm tingled. It happened a lot lately.

She mindlessly stroked the sleeve of the heavy suit in a soothing motion. Beneath, she knew every shape, every outline of the tattoo that started at the base of her neck and twisted down her left arm—a continuous patchwork of the visions behind her eyes.

For years, her mind had swatted at and grasped for infinite feelings, trying to capture them in her notebook—fragments of dreams, thoughts, and intuition that transformed into improbable shapes too complex for daylight.

Sitting in the chair, sweating, another dream flowed into her skin. The fire of the atomic age of rocketry became tendrils pulling at the nape of her neck, winding through the history of spaceflight—Mercury, Apollo, Luna, Muses. These were the colossal advances of a species reaching out to touch its nearest moon. But as history slowed, the images shifted. They were no longer from textbooks but from a future unwritten—a future only she could see.

Her mind continued to invent, bewitched as she slept: outlines of gorgeous mechanical birds with pearlesque eyes leaning, searching deep into the galaxy. Each epoch of a new space travel story flowed seamlessly into the next, etched down her arm.

When she was invited to join—a visual laureate among engineers, linguists, and cartographers—the images stretched to the back of her hand, filling every inch.

At first, she hid the markings. But with no privacy in space, she grew more comfortable with the questions. One by one, her crew noticed and remarked on how the intricate details she wore extended to the craft and equipment they now used. How could she have envisioned all of this over the years?

In her own way, she described the thoughts that inspired them, showing her crew the notebook—a chaotic rush of words and sketches. Some she could recall in vivid detail; others lingered only as ephemeral mist, caught between dream and sleep.

Now, she floated, the meandering Earth too far to touch. The space outside—and it really was space, not solely in the metaphoric sense—held a breadth of mystery cloaked in constant night.

Looking off, she was transfixed. How could you not be?

The stars didn't seem closer here—the nearest some 90 million miles away—but they were brighter in the black. For the last few days, she had watched the shapes continents spin by, their outlines often obscured by weather. The oceans, she learned, made the best reflective surface—so much so that the roundness of home appeared only as a hole punched in the dark.

Out here in the cold, she sometimes felt a constricting breathlessness for just a moment. With a deep swallow, she'd catch herself.

Her dreams in ink, stretching from her elbow to forearm, now surrounded her in metal and circuitry. But only time could divulge if the images, these dreams, once manifested only on her body before being made real would come true.

She wondered, as the constellations outside became unrecognizable, what delights lay beyond the infinite?

———

Music to read by:
Low Light - Peter Gabriel

GRAVITY

CHARLEEN WAILED TO THE SKY AS HER LOVE LAY DYING. SHE wept freely as the blood spread on its own, darkening the loose, mossy stones. His head—like Charleen's heart—had shattered into a thousand scattered pieces. For all the gallantry in the kingdom, no spell, no magic could reverse time and put him right.

Yet, quietly—beneath the soft crow of blackbirds in the orchard, beneath the buzzing of honeybees—she whispered in his ear... and lied.

In her heart—buried beneath regal wares and a padded corset that lifted her small breasts into something more— that pea-sized coal she called a heart, she knew he was dead. It panged only as much as she allowed.

"If he hadn't been such a daredevil," she thought—the blame a knee-jerk distraction, a missive from her darker, protective subconscious. But wasn't it pride she was shielding? Or was it?

Perhaps not.

As she watched his shape grow cold, his body twisted and uneven on the ground, she remembered how they'd met. Here. At this very spot, deep in the woods, where chance had first drawn them together.

Her horse, tired from a morning run, drank from the nearby stream as she wandered the orchard's edge. Beyond the stone wall, she heard the tapping of footsteps along the boundary.

A warbling, tangier-like whistle drew her eyes upward. And there he was—dressed in his finest outdoor attire, the gap in his wide smile shining down. He was far too young for a walking cane—jeweled or otherwise. And she remembered thinking, even then, that he was also too young to possess such riches. Yet there he stood, watching her with interest, unconcerned with her dowry.

It was in that instant, with him perched atop that wall, that she decided to turn his gaze into something more. She had set to wooing him—not the other way around.

So, she flirted. They walked, he atop the wall, she below. First, a few stolen minutes together. Then, hours lost along the boundaries of their respective kingdoms. She'd tuck sweets into her saddlebags, and he'd pick fruit from the treetops. But they had never touched. That would come only when retreat was no longer an option— for him. After all, free milk meant never being indebted to the cow.

Charleen recalled her first prediction: that sometime after their grand wedding—after the papers were signed, after the dowries transferred and the dust settled—he'd tumble down a flight of stairs or be found dead, a half-masticated piece of chicken lodged in his throat.

And then she'd be free to do... well, whatever she pleased.

But not like this.

So much for strategy. So much for patience.

She wiped the blood from her hands and whispered her final lie.

"Listen for hoofbeats," she said. "They're coming. All the King's horses, and all the King's men..."

It was, she supposed, the closest thing to mercy she could muster.

FREAKSHOW

BART was crowded and hot, everyone packed butts-to-nuts in the dank underground.

She brushed past the man and couldn't help but smile — that Cheshire-Cat-that-ate-the-canary kind of smile.

It was like electricity when it happened. Faster than a cranked-up electron. Instantaneous. The wave pulsed from her shoulder, up into her neck and down her spine.

She'd had the touch since she was a kid, but it wasn't until high school that she honed it—made it a silent skill. The wave would lift everything she needed, like a pickpocket of thoughts. And with one touch, she knew everything.

Unlike an average thief, her skills didn't require misdirection, sleight of hand, or prestidigitation. Sure, she could lift a wallet—like she just did—but she always came away with much more.

New York, Chicago, Atlanta, Austin, Phoenix, and now San Francisco — she'd been everywhere. She didn't look back anymore. Every city was just one more layer between her and the names that used to whisper freakshow in school hallways.

She exited into the Mission and let the smell of piss and bums wash over her. This wasn't her neighborhood. She never led a mark close to her place. She'd double back, skim the city until she was sure it was clean. The Mission made that easy — plenty of people, plenty of bars and dives to disappear into.

Rosamunde was dim and half-full. She dropped into a seat and ordered a La Fin Du Monde with the cash she pulled from the wallet.

Her mind flipped through the contents faster than her hands: library card — used once; Chase bank card — PIN two-six-one-eight, his lucky numbers; medical card — two prescriptions, migraines and Viagra; driver's license — expires on his forty-fifth birthday.

The layers of information sat right in front of her eyes, the cards just background noise now.

It's a gift, she thought. A horrible fucking gift, but one she couldn't do without.

She reached into the back pocket of the wallet, behind a wrinkled receipt for a frozen burrito. That's when she saw it — a cheap business card.

S.R. Detectives. Scribbled on the back: *Maria Karas, Lower Haight.*

Her thumb froze on the edge. He'd been looking for her. He'd almost found her.

They hadn't been this close to him in years—and she planned to keep it that way.

She stared at the card a beat longer. If only he knew—if her father understood that with just one touch, she could read him better than a book—would he feel any different about finding her?

She drained the last of the beer and slid off the stool, tucking the business card into her jacket pocket.

Outside, the light had gone soft and gold, bouncing off windows and pooling in the cracks of the sidewalk. She slipped into the street, head down, hood up.

A flash in a darkened window caught her eye. Glass doesn't lie.

A man. Two paces back. Holding a phone, but not reading it. His steps matched hers a little too well.

She didn't stop. Didn't look again. Just let her feet find the flow of the crowd.

The street swallowed her whole — bodies, voices, headlights flaring in the distance.

No panic. Just motion. Just instinct.

She moved like water, fluid and unseen.

And beneath it all, that grin tugged at the corner of her mouth.

She hadn't been chased in a while.

And she still remembered how to disappear.

———

Music to read by:
I'm Not A Woman, I'm a god - Halsey

———

Additional chapters written by fellow Substack authors:
https://tinyworlds.substack.com/p/freakshow

CRAIGSLIST

It's starting to feel like home here.

I wondered how it would all come to an end—a knife at my throat, a hit and run, maybe just enough drain cleaner in my evening cocktail. Something I'd never see coming.

We'd kiss goodnight in our matrimonial bed with threadbare sheets and roll our separate ways. I didn't expect to wake up. I told people that bitch would get me first.

The planning started innocently, the way you tell someone: *I wish he was dead.* Words hissed in exhaustion when the day is long.

How could I blame her, I'm hard to live with. It can't be easy. We're hard on each other. Difficult, I mean. That's what the shrink says I should say: we— *I* — am difficult to live with.

I can see her, typing her thoughts into Craigslist. She'd add a few choice descriptions about how she loathed me, how our life together was a joke. I bet she sold it real good.

It probably surprised her when someone answered the post—you know, a do-gooder with a hero complex. He was going to save her from the monster on the next pillow. He would tip the scale and right the ship. How dashing.

And she led him on, feeding him the little details that make all relationships sound rocky.

She probably started with the time I forgot her birthday, a line or two about my calm but nasty nature.

Then, I'll bet she set the hook with our drunken screaming outside the bar and her bloody lip at 3am.

It wasn't hard to get him interested.

I made sure of that.

I can see her reeling him in like a fish from a stocked pond.

Over the next month they probably plotted, talking about the life they'd have after. I remember seeing her at the computer late at night. I didn't think much of it then but remember it now.

And every day, I always woke up. Not so much as a hiccup as I sipped my late night bourbon.

I don't know how the police found out but they had been reading every email. They watched from afar until they had enough details.

The police knew how and when I would die. What a mindfuck, right?

Then the day came. We were both shocked when the badges showed up on the doorstep. With that awful tv show blaring they parted us in the living room shouting, guns drawn.

Through the open door I could see some guy sprawled out on the lawn, belly down and a cop on his back.

They made *her* sit on the couch but they handcuffed me. And that cocksucker detective told her about it all— Craigslist, the emails on her computer. Everything *I* had done.

All she could do was scream. Her eyes were wild, teeth biting in the air with each word.

That's the first time I truly saw hate in her eyes.

I'll tell you, she'd get me, if I didn't do it first.

It's all true, of course. Every word of it.

And this cell really is starting to feel like home.

55 WORD STORIES

I.

Hush," she said, watching.

He blinked, sweat coming, lie detector bleeping.

"I - I ..." his voice trailed off.

The lines swayed in the wrong direction.

A collective gasp.

Not a clink, not a fork moved.

The restaurant was still.

Her expression neutral,

then reversing,

gears grinding.

She closed the machine.

Three minutes in, a record.

There would be no second date.

2.

Every night before dawn
It's raining up
Grannies and infants and little boys
From neighborhoods, cities and vacant lots
From behind eyelids, above the pillow's
    warm side
Dreams and memories
Wishes and neverknowns in streams
Uprooted, plucked, released
Between particles of matter
Scattered
Can you feel them on the wind?

3.

Walter and Bennet stood back to back,
weapons poised.
"Twenty paces?" Walter asked.
Leather squeaked. Muscles tensed.
"As agreed," Bennet replied, inhaling deeply.
Onlookers gawked from an unsafe distance.
A dewy meadow silent, but for two.
Honor was to be restored
The day of reckoning had arrived.
Accordions At Dawn!

DISPATCHES

Musings from the Tiny Worlds universe. Mostly true.

C'MON LET HER ROLL

FROM DISPATCH NO. 16

A FULL YEAR BEFORE GRUNGE BROKE, JOHNNY CASH RELEASED the album *Boom Chicka Boom*.

Even though it was his 75th release and could've graced your collection, it probably didn't. And I can't offer some writerly absolution if you didn't notice it in the "nice price" bin.

Don't beat yourself up. I almost missed it, too...

But, let's say you **did** pick it up.

And before you left the cassette to melt on the dash of your car... you *would* have heard an unemotional if speedy version of Harry Chapin's *"Cat's in the Cradle"* and a farcical yet-likely-true tale written as a wink to a fellow Highwayman:

> *There were wackos and weirdos*
> *Dingbats and dodos*
> *and athletes and movie stars*
> *and David Allen Coe*
> *There was leather and lace*
> *And every minority race*

With a backstage pass
at the Willie Nelson show

Look, this album clearly wasn't crafted with care by the blue-collar poet laureate we recognize from Cash. I surmise that the Man in Black's wallet got a bit thin and he phoned it in for a few bucks.

I mean, even the title, *Boom Chicka Boom*, is simply an onomatopoeia of Cash's style, used ad-nauseam on every song.

But one track...

One song on that silly album got lodged in my brain, "*Monteagle Mountain.*"

In that ditty, Cash tells us in his singular style — half singing, half recitation — about the danger of driving a big rig over a steep mountain pass:

Goin' down Monteagle Mountain on I-24
   It's hell for a trucker when the devil's at your door
   He'll tempt you and tell you,
   "Come on, let her roll"
   'Cause the mountain wants your rig
   and trucker, I want your soul

It's just one of those songs, those ideas, that gets stuck in your crawl.

Fast forward a few years after *Boom Chicka Boom* lands with a collective *meh*, and I'm a 22 year old roadie living in Tennessee.

Between better-paying gigs, I wound up behind the wheel of a beat-up Mack truck, hauling stage gear from Chicago to Dallas to Atlanta—with Nashville as home base.

Truck drivers call it the Greenback Triangle. Nobody ever wrote a song about it—but it covers the rent.

The interview for transporting hundreds of thousands of dollars in equipment was about as thorough as a **carnival worker** might get: a gear-grinding test of that ancient MACK truck – a vehicle that hadn't seen a good day since it rolled off the assembly line — and a "turn and cough" medical test.

(*Yipee*, I'm a truck driver!)

I took to it quickly, I kind of still do, because I somehow identified with other truckers out there on the road–eating greasy food in the middle of the night and listening to strange tales told by Art Bell on the truck's AM radio. It's a strange existence.

After a late-night haul from Chicago, I pulled into the Nashville shop to swap gear for the next gig in Atlanta. Our semi-homeless crew took their sweet Southern time, while I studied a map of the route.

That's when I noticed something I hadn't considered—I'd have to go over... Monteagle Mountain.

Hmmm. Where had I heard that name before?

After eight hours from Chicago and another five to Atlanta, I'd be well past the regulated driving limit. No sweat, I had a tailgater stashed behind the bench seat (read: falsified). But that wasn't my main concern—it was the mountain.

I'd never driven over it before. I only knew it from that Johnny Cash song.

Tentatively, I began the long ascent up Monteagle. With a strong tailwind, the Mack truck could barely muster 60 mph. Now, climbing a 6% grade, it moved like honey in December.

Keeping it second gear—first would make it stall on a hill—I pondered Johnny's tune.

The western side was a climb, but which side was Cash singing about?

Was this the steep side, or the other? Maybe both?

Lumbering up the mountain, I took stock of my ride: balding tires that lost grip with just a light sprinkle, and steering that needed constant, vigorous correction making–less like driving and more like agitating a wash cycle.

Then my thoughts turned to the brakes—when had they last been serviced? **Ever**

When I finally crested the mountain a highway patrol checkpoint made every truck stop.

As we inched forward, our log books were scrutinized and inspectors poked around. When my turn came, they peered long and hard inside the cab.

"Air brakes?" one cop queried, noting my plate number.

"Air-assisted," I corrected, thinking of the nuances listed on my medical card compared to a full commercial drivers license.

"Where's the air warning light?" they pressed.

I was at a loss. It seemed plausible that the Mack was supposed to have such a feature—a lone bulb to signal trouble with the air-assisted brakes. I threw out a guess, not too convincingly, that maybe the old beast was from before such doohickeys became mandatory. This cop in the mirror shades wasn't buying it. He laid out my options: *go back to the truck stop to see about getting a light rigged up, or lay low until nightfall.*

"What happens at night?" I inquired.

Not looking up from his clipboard, he muttered, "Shift change."

Blinking against the late afternoon glare: *Had this lawman just subtly suggested when they might turn a blind eye?*

I decided to press my luck, "About what time?"

He didn't answer.

I meandered back to the truck stop to find the repair shop closed. That left me with one option: *wait.*

Quick math made me realize I'd be awake a full 24 hours before I got to Atlanta, most of it driving. But staying awake might not be the biggest problem–I'd have to traverse Monteagle at night.

Now, this was a time when the main method of communication consisted of a beeper and a pay phone.

I called to tell the boss I wouldn't make the load-in that evening, probably not until midnight or so. He was livid.

Even with the pay phone held away from my ear, the loudspeaker announcing, "Shower number 7 is ready," and the cacophony of the trucker arcade in the background, I swear I could hear the sound of his Dallas-coiffed mullet scratching, hoping to choke me through the receiver.

Over coffee and cigarettes, I found another driver who also knew the patrol stop would pack up at nightfall. I opted not to bring up the Johnny Cash song, but I did inquire about the side roads down Monteagle I'd seen on a map.

Through a haze of blue cigarette smoke, he laughed and said, "They're worse for a truck—narrow and steep. And," he leaned in, lowering his voice, "if the cops catch you bypassing the stop, there's no way you'll make it to Atlanta tonight."

At that I heard Johnny's voice again...

Yeah, many good man has lost his life
On Monteagle Mountain, it's a long steep grade
Many a good hard workin' boy gone over the side

I waited. And waited.

Veins buzzing with truck stop coffee, I steered back to the patrol stop where dozens of other rigs were marooned like castaways.

The open road, our rightful domain, teased us from just a few hundred feet away. There we sat, each of us marked with some petty infraction, like beaten dogs whining for the gate to swing open. We were the grizzled, sleep-starved outcasts of the asphalt.

And me, with a Cash-sized cloud over my head.

When the last patrol car vanished over the hill into the dark, our engines thundered to life.

As I joined the convoy, my hands gripped the wheel, slick with sweat, as the road plunged downward.

I switched on my hazards and hunkered to the right, letting the growl of the engine brake the descent.

Chain-smoking my way down, I lit each cigarette off the last's dying ember.

As the trucks barreled faster, and faster, our makeshift brigade formed a thundering wall of steel and rubber.

All the while, that haunting tune played like a soundtrack in my mind:

Goin' down Monteagle Mountain on I-24
It's hell for a trucker when the devil's at your door
He'll tempt you and tell you,
"Come on, let her roll"
'Cause the mountain wants your rig
and trucker, I want your soul

As I neared the base of Monteagle, my truck lagging behind schedule and racking up costs as stagehands waited for me in Atlanta, a thought struck me:

Where were the burnt-out shells of trucks from drivers who had "let her roll"?

Were they lost in the nighttime blur? Or had I, a novice driver, outmaneuvered death?

That was the moment it all clicked—the epiphany.

Damn.

No, I was not A.J. Foyt manhandling this oversized steering wheel. I'd been conned by one of the greatest showmen of all time.

He had pulled off the ultimate sleight of hand, and I'd fallen for it, hook, line, and sinker.

Throwaway album or not, Johnny Cash had done what he does best: spun a myth out of thin air.

I'd like to think I'm not the only driver who fell for it.

But, then again, I may be the only person you'll meet who remembers the album *Boom Chicka Boom*.

KNIVES OUT

FROM DISPATCH NO. 18

For a short while I dated a woman I met online—you know, through one of those apps. One afternoon we met up for a walk and I asked what she did that morning.

Her reply, "I took a class working on my knife skills at the CIA."

I think I paused or my pace stumbled a bit as I took in the words. I mean, she *was* a bit secretive about what she did for a living. Maybe knife training was just the sort of thing an agent might do. After all, while online dating I had met people who worked in all sorts of fields—a film editor, a (few) startup founders, even a lawyer for the Department of Homeland Security. So, maybe a CIA agent wasn't out of line?

I imagined her sparring with an attacker, disarming them with John Wick-style finesse. She certainly seemed the type.

The further we walked, though, I started to wonder if I'd misheard her. It had certainly happened to me before when I followed a colleague through the streets of Taipei looking for a soup shop. When pressed, he told me they made *"custom soups, anything you want, ready in a couple of days"* For nearly an hour we traversed Taipei's alleyways, side roads and down a set of rickety stairs to a small doorway where inside stood a man who did indeed make custom things: suits.

I rebooted my ears and did a system check. Was she speaking clearly? *Yes.* Do I understand her words? Again, *yes.* Am I going deaf? *No.*

So, I asked, "The CIA?"

She responded in the affirmative.

"Do you... take classes there a lot?" I asked.

"Sometimes, to sharpen my skills" she answered, "but they're so expensive."

We walked and talked for a while but I couldn't get it out of my head—are agents, ones with combat training, supposed to tell you this kind of thing? I thought about how sometimes people blather nervously on first dates and tell you their entire life story—almost always TMI and in rapid-fire style—but she didn't do that and this wasn't a first date.

I decided to broach the topic one last time, "I'd think the CIA wouldn't make you pay for those classes, like, it would just be part of training or something."

She stopped, tilted her head to the side, eyebrows widened like looking at a puppy that can't find its way out of a box and said, "Culinary Institute of America."

WHISPERS & DREAMS

I'LL OFTEN STOP AT THE SIDE OF THE ROAD JUST TO GAWK.

This a view of the northwestern side of Mt. Shasta, only a few miles from a co-op farm where my family spends time. The photos were taken in March, before the plains turn green, the grasses trying once again to overtake the stone ballast beneath the tracks.

It looks lonely out there.

Looks deceive.

Maybe you can imagine a wind that flows steady and unyielding over the hills and down to the lowlands—like honey in the summer and bitter in winter.

It isn't lonely, though. It whispers of history, and of dreams that stayed behind.

I've heard about trappers arriving wild-eyed at these new lands.

Timber cooperatives fashioned with a handshake—with sweat, they's pull Douglas fir or pine from high in the mountains for sprawling cities further south.

Moonshiners, too, some pulling juniper berries from the forest, chasing a wilder kind of spirit.

Cattle ranchers, who have owned that land for generations, would fill it with thousands of heads. And there will be spring calves jumping, suckling, and bawling.

Some of those fields would turn a crop—alfalfa or barley.

The railroad tied them all together. It still does, in some ways. The ballast beneath those iron rails once bore the weight of steam and ambition.

First they carried timber and stone, carving roads through the wilderness. Then came the great passenger lines, winding across the land, stitching distant towns into one country. Depots bustled with cattlemen, loggers, and families chasing new beginnings. In time, freight took over —grain, mail, fuel—all rumbling south and west.

Now the trains still pass, smaller, quieter, but following the same ribbons laid down long ago.

And the land still hums with their passing—whispering of all the lives that once moved through here, and of the dreams that never left.

THE ESCAPE

FROM DISPATCH NO. 23

"Forty miles up the road," the man in the red flannel said, his eyes locked onto mine. I knew—somewhere deep down—that this place, a mile or so from the Mexican border, could be where it ended.

Then, his whisper came, barely audible: *Go.*

I left Nashville two days earlier on my motorcycle, braving ten-degree weather with a windchill hovering around minus twenty. Barely three hours into the ride, I stopped at a gas station near Memphis and called my then-wife.

"What the fuck have I done?" I remember asking, my voice lost in the cold.

This ride wasn't just a journey—it was almost a dare: a fast westward push, a long southern arc, then a final swing north into Las Vegas. Even in January, I knew the desert sun would be warm enough to melt away the winter blues.

But the freezing temperatures across Arkansas and down into Texas didn't ease up. It wasn't until I reached Greenville, Texas, that I found any warmth—inside a dim bar where a dollar bought me a "membership" to drink in this partially wet town. The next morning, I woke to a layer of ice covering my bike and another day of temperatures stuck in the teens. The rain, when it wasn't turning to sleet, came down steadily. I pushed on, looking at the world through a foggy visor, the cold seeping through my discount heated gear and into my bones. The miles blurred together as I rolled through Fort Worth, Abilene, and Odessa, each town passing like a shadow in the cold.

By mid-afternoon, as I reached the southernmost stretch of the journey, the sun finally leaned over the flatlands, bringing with it a welcome warmth. But with that warmth came a fierce wind, rising from the south like an ancient force. It billowed over the plains, pushing against me, leaning my bike as I fought to keep it upright and straight on the open road.

It's in these moments that the mind starts to spiral downward:

Can I survive this?

Where'd that truck go?

I'm definitely going to die out here.

But I pressed on. After enough miles, a bond forms between rider and bike—you come to know every wobble, every sputter. You learn when the shocks need adjusting, how the tire treads are wearing, and how much fuel is left— even before the warning light comes on (if you have one). You learn these things because your survival depends on it. Feeling the bike's changes—its subtle shifts—is the differ- ence between making it or not.

And, in a way, the bike knows you, too. It senses when you're tired, when hunger sets in, and when visibility fades as the sun drops below the horizon, plunging you into civil twilight where contrast disappears and obstacles hide in the dark. The bike speaks, if you're listening, telling you when it's time to rest before it bucks you off into the scrub or throws you sideways into a pole. It knows, and it's your job —your life—to know it, too.

My strength faltering, my bladder full, and my tank nearly empty, I pulled into the dirt parking lot at a gas station. The station lights hadn't been turned on yet—a detail I took to mean they hadn't noticed night was only a few minutes away. But as I pulled up and threw down the kickstand, I saw the pumps were rusted hulks, each hose torn away. I looked again at the gas light on my bike, lit a dozen or so miles back, signifying I was running on reserve —fumes.

"Fuck..." I muttered, looking around. In my tired state, I reasoned that the few cars in the parking lot were safety enough to get off the bike, leaving all my belongings strapped to it.

I walked toward the store, hoping for a bathroom, some warmth, maybe directions, too. Inside, the place was even more desolate than the outside suggested. A few drivers lingered at old, chipped tables, their eyes down. The deli counter held only a couple of shriveled sausages, and the man behind it watched as I walked in, his eyes following my every move. The overhead lights flickered, casting shadows that made everyone's faces look ghostly. Living, then not.

I rounded the corner to the bathroom, where two men, startled by my entrance, quickly turned and walked past me. Peeling off a long-distance motorcycle suit takes time, and as I did, I could hear the low murmur of voices just beyond the wall. The sound carried, impossibly clear, even with the echo in the bathroom—conspiratorial, halted, but never above a whisper. I listened for the sound of a door chime, expecting the men who left so abruptly to be making their exit, like I planned to do soon. But I never heard it. Nor did I hear the clatter of plates, coffee cups, or even the drone of a TV. The people I had seen earlier—drivers lingering at tables—seemed frozen in place. But why?

I glanced at myself in the dingy mirror: matted hair, road grime streaked across my neck. As I looked closer, something about my suit caught my attention. The reflective stripes on my shoulders and arms—they looked official. And then it hit me. My gear: black helmet with a symbol on the side. My bike: a black Honda ST, the kind often used by police departments across the country.

Did I look like a cop? Was there something illegal happening here, and did they think the damn police had just walked in on it?

My heart pounded, and my hands fumbled with the zipper as I stepped out of the bathroom. I kept my eyes down, struggling with the jacket, when the man from behind the counter moved into my path. He was tall, with a lumberjack build and a red flannel shirt, blocking me in the space near the front door.

"Gas?" I asked, finally looking up at him.

"Forty miles up the road," he replied, his gaze locked onto mine, unblinking. Out of the corner of my eye, I noticed others in the room—people I hadn't seen before. Some stood, while others sat at tables, all of them watching me in silence.

Then, his mouth moved, no sound escaping. Just a single word: *Go.*

The ground seemed to shift under my feet as I moved, my hands fumbling for gloves that were too wet to pull free. I fished out my keys, the motorcycle engine roaring to life as the gas light flickered yellow again—how many miles did I really have left?

I yanked my helmet on, and that's when I heard them—two men shouting at me. Their words were lost in the noise as the bike rumbled beneath me, feeling lighter than it had all day. My back wheel spun in the loose dirt below the pumps, kicking up dust as I gunned it, fighting the urge to look back.

In the mirror, I saw them throwing something—rocks? Cans? I couldn't tell. The bike wobbled as I hit the pavement and shot up the overpass, my grip tightening on the bars. I glanced over my shoulder at the gas station; its lights were no brighter than when I'd pulled up minutes ago. Adrenaline sharpened my focus, and through that clarity, I saw the place for what it was—derelict, isolated, and now fading fast behind me.

The bike and I tore down the interstate, our two beings fused into one as the adrenaline surged. The boundary between man and machine vanished; my pulse in sync with the engine's hum.

We skimmed along the asphalt, the bike inhaling the last vapors from the tank, propelling us forward. Every mile felt like a gamble, the road stretching endlessly ahead, but I kept the throttle steady, trusting the bike to carry us just a little farther—knowing that, in this moment, *our* survival depended on moving as one.

When I finally stopped, some miles down the road in the full light of a working gas pump and a police station across the street, I filled the tank—7.6 gallons in a 7.7-gallon tank. We were both running on fumes.

In Las Cruces, beer in hand, the adrenaline finally faded. But the memory didn't. That gas station—its darkened pumps, its motionless watchers—kept coming back.

Maybe they were just strung-out locals. Maybe it was nothing.

But even now, riding at night, whenever I pass a place too quiet, too dimly lit, I still hear that whisper behind my visor.

Go.

STORIES

The smaller the world, the stronger the pull.

Funny how that works.

THE WINDOW

"I believe I've looked through thousands of windows before," he said, his mouth agape, "but none has ever been quite like this."

In the quiet of the room, I stood back as he circled, creating an arc from one side of the window to the other. He was studying it, looking at every detail along its frame, the reflection of the desk lamp behind us, and through the glass to the image on the other side.

He held a hand up, reaching to touch it when I stopped him, grasping his wrist with a light but purposeful hand.

"My only request is we mustn't touch the window," I said, letting go.

His hand hung momentarily in the air before retreating to his pocket, his face angled toward me but not at me, to ask, "What happens if it's touched?"

To this question, I could not answer fully. I probed the theories in my mind, the memory of those I'd written in my notebook full of equations and footnotes.

"I have some ideas, but none fully proven. Best leave it alone until I can provide a more scientific test."

And with this answer, he seemed satisfied, still not averting his eyes from the image that lay just beyond the glass and frame. For there, the image that he saw was not one I put there but one his mind conjured all on its own. Though I've long looked into it, I could not have chosen what his image would be; that was for him the reason to keep watching.

When he had stared for a sufficient amount of time, I asked what he saw. To this, he merely burbled a few words, "My poor mother, the lightness then, of floating freely." His thoughts in word form were a mix of emotion and the state of the imagery. They were just as mine were when I first looked into the window.

Not more than a week ago, I had completed work on the frame—mechanisms of wire and current—and was grinding the last edges of the glass. You see, it's a multi-part construction like that of a fresnel lens but without the chromatic aberrations—a truly perfect plane for seeing, well, whatever the viewer thinks of.

In my first tests, I saw in the window a young man so fraught with anxiety that he hid under his bed, crying. Of course, I could not see the entire bed nor the room, but I recognized just a decorative edge of the duvet, which dangled to the floor in front of the boy. And I saw his eyes, filled with tears, and a bit of his school uniform, the crest of a Starling sitting atop oak leaves. These details, deduced in a matter of seconds, led me to recognize the boy was me. It was the first day of class at boarding school, and I was so dreadfully frightened of being away from home that I hid for the whole day beneath the bed.

In subsequent tests, I saw other things—my adolescent self standing over a dying bird fallen by a stone from my hand. Or another moment when I sat in the rose garden weeping after my mother had passed. Each was seen as through a telescope or with some other magnification not yet invented.

The man here, standing agape at the window now, sees something else at that same distance. He watches the shadows and shapes of a child, a foetus, still in the womb. The eyes of the child open and close, as do the fists. The skin, so delicate in the embryonic fluid, is almost translucent. As the light shifts, perhaps the mother reading by candlelight, we can see the child's heartbeat under the still-forming ribs. We can see the arc of the spine subtly as we move with parallax to the edge of the frame.

And all these movements, just the same as when I saw my own self hiding under the bed, the eyes of this child follow us. The window, as my tests now confirm, is two-way. But what, if anything, can the subject inside the pane see? Are we apparitions clearly visible to them? I do not have any recollection from my own childhood of seeing such things, but the memories of those moments are so far in the past, can I be sure of it?

I pick up my laboratory notebook to jot down these thoughts. My hands are shaking with excitement and pulsing with anticipation of the further tests I will perform. I shall take the time to scour my memory for moments where I may have seen things unexplained and irrational. I note on a new page the spectre that lurked by my window as a child, its shadows falling from the tree outside when, in daylight, there were only twisted branches and tangles of moss.

But what, my mind turns, of these moments seen in the window, are they only of sadness or fright? Could they not be ones of immense joy? Surely our lives are full of these moments that they brim forth most easily?

I search my memory of the hours spent in quiet contemplation of the device, of the meticulous placement of each cog, each spark. In this design, I can find no fault in its systems.

As the window is meant to reflect our emotions, our memories, I realize the problem. Like a scent that lingers on our clothes, some memories of our past are never far from mind. And the ones hidden but most close to the surface, so indelibly etched, are the traumas we have yet to wrestle. No, I resolve, the issue with the window is not a mechanical one, not one of construction or materials. The error is human.

I am awakened from this daydream by a horrible crash. The man, fallen to the ground, taking with him some of my instruments on the nearby bench. In the clatter of it, I see him curl on the ground, his eyes open, his mouth still agape. My hands, trembling with my own excitement, reach for him, hoping to right him. But I find that his eyes and pulse are becoming more still by the second. I call out for help and hear heavy steps coming from the next room where my assistant works. She shrieks as she enters, the man on the floor, me draped over him. But her eyes are on the window.

Looking up, I see a watery ripple in the scene and the embryonic fluid rushing down and out of the window. I look to the man's hand and see that it is covered in the same; his suit jacket is wet. In the window, I see the child, still in the womb, begin to close its eyes. Under the translucent skin, the heart slows further and further until all movement stops.

My assistant holds herself on the door frame, sobbing uncontrollably, as I stand.

have no words to describe to her what has transpired. Could I find them, conjure them out of thin air, I'm not certain they would make sense.

But in that moment—and in the ones that followed—I was resigned to sink it to the bottom of the ocean and never look into it again.

Days later, I boarded a boat, the window wrapped in velvet. I instructed the captain to sail to the deepest part of the ocean we could reach in a day. He did so, though with a measure of hesitation.

When we arrived, I heaved the window over the side. From my hands it tumbled, the rope fraying as it dropped through the waves. Though I had bound the cloth tightly, the fall and current stripped it away.

And as it sank, I looked one last time through the glass.

My own face stared back—not as a child, but as a young man, consumed by study, so ghostly in presence I'd nearly disappeared. There was no fear in that face. Only the bright confidence of someone who believed, with absolute conviction, that he would one day invent a machine to transform man—to reshape perception enough to alter history.

That confidence was real. I remember it. I felt it again in that moment, standing at the rail.

The window worked exactly as I had hoped.

But I did not see then—what I see now: It should never have been built.

———

Music to read by:
The Heart Asks Pleasure First - Michael Nyman

TWO PALMS MOTEL

WRITTEN WITH JASON THOMPSON

DOWN SOME STRETCH OF BUSTED-UP ASPHALT, YOUR RAGTOP flies.

The sun has tumbled off the edge of the earth, throwing molten slag into the clouds. Night might be coming, but that hellish wind needling your skin and eyes for the last few hours will never quit.

At best, your Spanish is rusty but the norteño station, riding shotgun since Vegas, has you tapping along. Everything is a whirl of nonsense, so why not the music, too?

Shaking your head, hoping the road comes into focus, doesn't help.

The weeklong bender and those dead brain cells are the only take-home in that doggie bag brain of yours. Luckily, you escaped with something more tangible.

Through the fog you remember that Navy swinger everyone called Battleship. He says the place where the sea meets the sky is called the offing. You see that now as the road and sky merge into a tunnel of nothingness.

There it is, you have found the offing.

So, with an ashtray full of butts and yours melted to the vinyl seat, you pull off, welcomed by the skeletal husks of long-dead palm trees and a dirt parking lot.

A trio of motorcycles sit idling, their Milwaukee aspirations ready for a quick departure, in front of a dozen rooms facing the highway. To everyone, this place is a pit stop somewhere between Hell and Oblivion.

To call it kitschy would be a lie–it's a shithole.

No matter, your internal gauge is on *E*. Any remaining miles will have to wait.

A night watchman doesn't look you in the eye as you push a couple of twenties at him. You're thankful he's glued to the titty magazine for two reasons: you'd have to smell his breath directly instead of ricocheted off the countertop, and he might recognize you—from another life, on page thirty-two.

The metal number on the door says nine, but when the lock breaks free, a nail holding it disintegrates. Sliding in a sad downward arc, the number spins: now it's room six.

It strikes you as funny that in an instant, things can receive a new identity. Entropy is magnificent, innit? You blink, banking that thought for another day–maybe in a new life.

Before you enter, you know this place is a murder scene with the bodies only recently carted away. A lone bulb sends a search beam ahead of you, a warning beacon, telling the cockroaches to arm themselves—tonight might just be a fight!

Travelers have shuffled the shag carpet thin, and the sun has leached the color to something best described as distressed carrot–the least favorite Sherwin Williams color. You remind yourself to keep your boots on as glass crunches under your feet.

Two twin beds wrapped in a fitted sheet occupy the center. Judging by the giant Rorschach blotch, there's a very real chance this bedding was *never* new.

Stains on the walls are deviant, deep, and honest. They're from years of unbathed souls seeking shelter.

Like you, these walls have history, too—not the kind written in pastel-colored textbooks, but rather carved with knives into the doorjamb, the plaster, the headboard, like:

The invitation: Souls for sale, inquire within
The rebuke: Fuck MJP!
The advertisement: Sandy gives good head

Dropping your bag, you stretch, letting your spine unroll — you've spent too many hours crouched, looking in the rearview, watching each vibrating speck on the horizon.

You're too hungry to eat. It's A strong drink-or-bust kind of night.

The bottle tips back easily. Too easily.

Here's to the offing you think, as the liquid in the bottle swishes its medicinal march toward your veins.

In the quiet heat, you remember how you greased the bookie setting the trap.

How you found the cop who would play nice for a sloppy favor. But mostly you remember him—his mouth agape like some prehistoric fish dragged from the deep. He'd been rooked, and you were the architect.

Good riddance.

The fucker deserved nothing and got it.

You remember laughing, throwing the bag in the car, twisting the key, and peeling away. The zipper broke when you hit the curb and a thousand Franklins stared dead-eye at you from the floorboards.

Now, here in the twisted nowhere of this place, nobody ever asks for a fresh pot of coffee or when the workout room opens. The lives of people who stop here are secret; their troubles are their own.

That's how it's meant to be, isn't it?

Welcome to The Two Palms Motel, where there's always a vacancy.

————

Music to read by:
Agua Turbia - Guadalupe Plata
Santo Enterrio - Guadalupe Plata

JOHATSU

Listening to my car idle, I think about petrol in the tank, imagining the engine casually pulling coins from my purse as it sips. It's a simple exchange I accept of more-or-less equal forces. But if I press the accelerator and speed through the streets, this moment of equilibrium is lost – harmony falls out of balance, disrupted.

I think about this, and other things, as I wait below an expensive high rise at the spine of Nakano and Toshima. I'm to drive him—it's most always a man—to Ikebukuro. A smaller station is nearby but large stations are best for anonymity.

Our eyes make contact in the rearview mirror as he steps in. Some are surprised by a woman, but he is not. I say nothing, but he nods slowly—a customary bow, a gesture I do not return. His reddened, watery eyes drift to the street outside, then to the building above. I see him searching for his balcony. Perhaps he is hoping for one last look. I'm not meant to know why he's leaving, but do.

He has a small satchel — we specify one shoulder bag, nothing more. His bag likely carries clothes and a few keepsakes. The trinkets will carry the heaviest weight, a constant reminder that his lover woke to an empty apartment.

My car moves through the wet, early morning streets when traffic is light. A patter of rain mixes with road noise but does little to mask his sobbing, which comes in waves as we drive deeper into the city. Most cry, as he does now. Some loudly wail while others pretend not to cry but their eyes and their short, shallow breaths are telltale.

My car is as anonymous as it is safe and in the crying I offer no outward emotion, only a quiet transit—one dot on the map to another.

I see him glance at his ticket, already purchased and waiting on the seat. The train will take him as far as Odawara. After that, I don't know his destination. Through the mirror I watch reflections of the city glide over his face while a film of the past plays behind his eyes. He says nothing as he exits the car and disappears into the station. I tap an update on my phone and drive away, my job completed.

———

"Sumimasen," I say, barely a whisper.

Haruto mumbles his own apology, stepping aside to let me pass. If he looks in my direction at all, it's through me. His face is still a paper mask where all color has run off the edges. He has been wandering, shuffling through the minutes between sundowns. To him, everyone is an apparition.

I step by, averting my eyes, proper. Though, I want to look at his face, to stare like tourists with lingering eyes, taking in all the details. I want to look for signs of change, but it's too soon. The ghost he most often looks for will never return home, will never wrap her arms around him. She's been gone only a few weeks, not nearly a month.

Was my bump intentional? I can't remember if I was thinking about balance or equilibrium again. The imagined sound of clinking weights on a metal scale makes me think it was balance—as if anything could provide a counter-weight. If he were to break down, here, on the floor of the market, would I step forward, bending a knee to help? Or, would I turn away as the clerks help him up and dust off his clothes? I honestly don't know.

Every other day, I see him picking out a few items for dinner, his daughter, Rin, by his side. She says hello and babbles her questions at me, at everyone that walks by. To her I'm no more special than the others in the store, and not as special as the sweet she might get if she's behaved.

I watch her fingers stray along the fruit—apples and bananas—until they linger on the colorful, bumpy dragon fruit. I want to hand one to her, to open it and taste the sweet fruit right there in the aisle. But I can't.

I watch her cry when Haruto doesn't put one in his shopping basket. She sobs as they walk home. I follow for a while until our paths separate.

———

Rin and Haruto are at the park, as they do every few days. She has on a new dress and is twirling. Sometimes I see her whisper from behind her father, not eager to mix with the other children. But today she is exuberant, playful, beautiful.

In the picture I have, Rin is much younger. Her hair has not yet grown to length. Haruto is full of life as he smiles at the camera in a way I can only imagine it might. At the playground, his face is still slack, but he's putting on a smile for her, eyes wide with mock excitement. It's been three months now, and I can see he is still missing an invisible limb. I imagine him at night, turning in bed to find her pillow cold, the sheets crisp. Then, I imagine him turning again, but this time he finds me lying there. I don't imagine anything after that first touch.

The other person in the picture with Rin and Haruto is Sana. She still has weight on her face from being pregnant, though the child is almost a year old. Her makeup is clean, but dark circles under her eyes are unmistakable. Her smile seems forced, an affectation of happiness. I study her and wonder if she is then, in the photo, thinking about leaving.

In my makeup mirror, I look at my own face. Our mouths are similar, Rin's and mine. If not my own daughter, then maybe a family resemblance. I look again; maybe our brows are alike, too?

———

A teetering, unsettling feeling is never far from my thoughts as I drive, like a sinkhole opening and into it slips all light, all happiness. How long have I felt like this?

During corona, work was plentiful, when constant proximity made lies almost impossible to hide—like gambling away family savings. Or when a lover, appearing suddenly at the doorstep at night, could no longer be hidden.

In truth, I don't know how to feel for the ones who disappear. How could I, of all people, criticize the disgraced when I am the getaway driver? Night movers, like me, can offer only johatsu—the desperate act of vanishing. Our clients are relocated far from home, for a fee, to start anew. I am told we can no more judge them than we can hide the truth.

I once asked if anyone changes their mind. Another grunted, "No."

"Does anyone ever return home?" I probed, as far as I dared.

"Trust, once lost, cannot be regained," was the answer.

And when I hear the silent or loud cries in the back seat of my car, I know the pain is real for them. Secretly, though, I take some comfort that shame cannot be absolved, no matter the price.

But what about those who remain?

————

Carelessly left behind, three faces with new family smiles look up at me from the floor of the car. I'm not meant to know the client's name, but the back of the photo reads plainly: Haruto, Sana, Rin.

With dry eyes, Sana calmly stared out the window as we drove. I deposit her at Shibuya station. She doesn't look back at the car, as most do. I turn the corner, out of sight, to remove any traces of the client from the vehicle. It's there that I find the picture.

Some kind of darkness fills my throat when I think of her. It's here that the image of unbalance begins to take shape. In my mind is the shifting of a scale: one platform suddenly empty and the weights of the other falling to the table.

————

My tea is cool to the touch, mirrored by the snow falling outside—a rare treat. Traffic and trains will be delayed. I think of these things often as I must chart an optimal course for clients.

But tonight, my mind is preoccupied after overhearing Haruto's abstract explanations to Rin about her mother's departure.

"She was sick," he says.

"Can doctors help?" Rin asks, the innocent hope of return not yet drifting away.

Haruto pauses, then shakes his head. I see on his brow the heft of Sana's shame.

His eyes are reaching for, trying to grasp everything quickly, to box it and bury it forever, so Rin remains clean. Somehow he knows though, like I do, in time she will uncover it. But, please, not yet.

I wonder if he knows Sana's demons are not his own? Questions without answers are the burden for those left behind.

I think of this unbalance as I pull the picture of Sana, Haruto, and Rin from a drawer. Around it are other artifacts left in my car—a bank note, a wedding band, a pair of glasses.

Then I see what I've really come for, my own photo. In it I am smiling, my fiancé is making a silly face. I remember the photographer's flash and the exact moment. We are happy, in love, our wedding only a few days away. But before it, my fiance is gone. He is one of the johatsusha, the disappeared.

In his place are the questions I still can't answer fully. I know these same questions weigh on Haruto's mind, felt on his brow and in the emptiness of his bed, even now, as snow falls outside his window.

————

"Rin," I hear Haruto call out when she's strayed too far.

He approaches as I'm knelt down talking to her. He sees she is safe and offers me a simple, "Arigatou."

Though he has often been too consumed to notice, this has been our meeting place—the grocery, with its narrow aisles and proximity to our houses.

I stand and smile. It's been almost a year, and Rin is talking quite well. Haruto, too, has shed his paper facade, his smile warm as he looks at me.

"Haruto," he says, bowing.

I return the bow. "Miyu," I say.

And, with a heartbeat of time, I look down to the little girl standing between us and say, "You are Rin?"

She smiles broadly, taking the dragon fruit from my hand and holding it up for him to see.

I think of balance again and how our scales may never be level with unanswered questions lingering just out of reach. And how shame can rot us from the inside without any visible signs.

Then, I consider how subtle the forces of time and patience are in offering their own counterbalance—as a salve slowly heals a wound. Maybe life is never in balance at all, but always, like a tide, working toward an unseen equilibrium.

————

Music to read by:
The Benefit of Hindsight by Nolan Green

THE BEAR

Late at night, around the full moon, a bear joins me for tea. I'm still getting used to it.

I suspect you're wondering how a bear can manage a teacup. The answer is—well, it's not exactly a teacup. I'll get to that shortly.

After long days of writing I'm often awoken by characters jabbering until the wee hours. These semi-frequent bouts of insomnia find me outside with a cup of tea. I've tried almost everything to get back to sleep, but only the sound of crickets, the night creatures, and a cup of tea seem to work.

Recently, a hulking figure emerged from the woods. His broad shoulders and lumbering gait came through my wife's hedges, trampling the hydrangeas and boxwood. I'd always thought bears were noisy, but this one moved in near silence. Startled, I watched him sniff the air, his graying muzzle pointed skyward.

Clearly, a scent had captured his attention... until I realized, as he looked in my direction, it was my rooibos. I like it because it's soothing, but the bear found it irresistible—a blend from the local shop, it carries earthy, honey-like notes with hints of vanilla and fruit. He sidled up to the porch, lightly clawing at the stairs. In a panic, I set my cup down, ran inside and watched through the kitchen window as he tipped it over and lapped the warm tea from the decking.

The next evening, before the voices woke me, he left a small package—a twist of sticks and bark—on my back stoop. He was seemingly apologizing for his abrupt entrance. It wasn't until I turned it over that I realized it was an ornamental sculpture of the two of us, he at the bottom of the stairs on the ground, and me at the top, each holding a teacup. I was taken aback, not just by its fine detail (which it certainly had), but by the likeness—down to my striped housecoat. But there was no mistaking the tableau, and no mistaking the intent: this bear was inviting himself for tea.

What could I do but entertain the idea?

The next night, I started the kettle while regularly peering out the window for signs of the bear. I began to wonder, perhaps especially in my insomnia-induced state, how we would greet each other if he appeared. I needn't have worried.

As I carried the accoutrements—teacups, carafe, and sweeteners on a tray—and put them on the table outside, I heard a deep, throaty huff from below. Trembling, I set down the tray and saw the bear, sitting at the bottom of the stairs. Just as the carving depicted, his sizable frame rose nearly halfway up the steps from the garden below.

With one arm leaned on the middle tread, he looked up at me. By the light of the recently full moon, I could see him clearly—his strong muzzle framing a mouth full of razor-sharp teeth, his dark eyes fixed on me, and his large arm (if that's what they're called) resting in a relaxed state, forearm to paw spanning the width of the step.

But there was something else, something I hadn't expected. He looked at me, then at the moon, directing my gaze, and said with a deep rasp, "You're a gracious host for having me on such a beautiful night. Thank you."

I couldn't help but laugh out loud at the absurdity of it all—a bear and I, about to have tea together! Perhaps you would have done the same? Shaking, I proceeded to serve. Before pouring, I turned and asked, attempting to hide my nervous but wide smile, "How do you take it?"

He responded, almost apologetically, "Just a bit of honey, if you have some." I did, as that's how my wife prefers her tea as well.

Reflecting on the size of the cup and the bear's paw, I excused myself to the house for a moment but returned as quickly as I could.

"I'm at a loss for a cup of your size," I said to the bear, "Perhaps one of these will do?"

The bear examined the various cups and mugs I brought out. He regarded them carefully, sometimes placing his paws on either side to gauge the size. He settled on a bucket-like tub we sometimes use for chicken fat. Holding it gingerly between both paws, he lifted it, pantomimed drinking from it, then placed it back on the step with a satisfied huff of approval.

I set about preparing his tea in the, *erm*, tub, and my own as well. To ease the awkwardness, I attempted some small talk.

"Do you often have tea with, um, humans?"

He huffed several times in a high-pitched staccato. Was that a laugh?

"You're the first," he said, "but I've thought about it many times."

Tea in hand, *er*, paw, we sat—the bear on the grass below and I on the top step—and sipped our tea by moonlight.

During that first official meeting, I learned the bear's name was Walter. Owing to his lack of tongue dexterity, I had to ask several times, apologetically, to understand him. "Water," it sounded at first. We exchanged pleasantries, inquiring about each other's families, how long we had lived in the area, and, of course, our thoughts on the tea. This was all quite civil, like we happened upon each other at the local diner and exchanged pleasantries.

When he finished, Walter set the tub gently on the step and licked his lips. He huffed, nearly a sigh, and looked at the waning crescent moon, then at me.

"Thank you. May I come back tomorrow?" he said finally.

"Yes!" I squeaked.

He nodded before lumbering off the way he had come.

This is how most nights ended. Sometimes there was more fanfare as he caught a scent on the wind and hurried off in its direction. In these cases, he would apologize the next day for his abrupt exit to chase down dinner or an after tea snack by appearing with a gift. Dangling from his mouth he'd bring an elegant weave of oak and maple leaves containing several handfuls of delicious local berries.

Not knowing how long these visits would last, I decided to write down a few questions for my new friend. I also took the opportunity to ask others about bears in the area. It seemed Walter was a black bear—by all accounts a mostly skittish, dumpster-diving local. He had been seen foraging for whatever he could find: insects, berries, fish, and remnants left behind at the campsites on the edge of town. Armed with a legal pad full of questions, I eagerly awaited his next visit—but Walter didn't appear.

As the nights grew darker, the moon waning to a sliver, then disappearing, there was still no sign of Walter. Night after night as my new novel languished, the voices quiet, I slept more regularly. Though I still kept a tea tray ready just in case. Some two weeks passed before I saw him again, I almost forgot. My insomnia had returned and I was awake, tea in hand.

"Seth!" he said as he finally trundled through the bushes. I startled, nearly knocking my own tea to the ground, as I had almost fallen asleep, the warm air and sounds of summer lulling me back to bed.

"Walter!" I said.

I scurried inside, filling the kettle full and readying the serving tray. As the kettle was warming I stuck my head outside and said, "snack?" Walter grunted, I took this as a yes and set up another small tray of crackers and cheese.

Placing his tea and snacks on the step Walter looked at me. Then, he set a quite heavy paw down, the size of it covering the whole of my foot.

"Gibbous moon starts tonight," Walter said. I didn't take his meaning but followed his stare.

"Ah, yes, the first quarter!" I said.

Walter sighed and nearly whispered, "All the world's magic is now available."

We both stopped moving for a few minutes as we looked up to the moon making its slow arc. The transit here was quite beautiful as we were surrounded by the buzzing of the night insects and the moon's soft glow.

There was something in his look that made me wonder who or what I was being visited by. Could this be an apparition of my own making? Is Walter for real or part of a latent insomnia-induced insanity?

Walter did not apologize for his absence, as it wasn't

necessary, but I began to note the days he appeared—always, from the first quarter through the full moon, ending at the last of the waning gibbous.

That night and the next few leading to the full moon Walter was quite talkative. He told me about the cubs he had grown up with and their extended families. It was intriguing to learn about the various bears in the area, many of whom he hadn't seen since they were quite small. Though he admitted his pack didn't travel far, roaming only a few miles throughout the day, some had taken leave to other parts of the countryside enchanted by stories about rivers full of fish and valleys of wild berries. Walter, it seemed, did not share in their wanderlust.

When I inquired why not he only answered with a low grumble. But something about that stuck with me so the next night I broached the topic again, though hesitantly, "Why not travel out to find your own parcel?"

Walter sipped his tea but did not answer.

"I don't mean to intrude, of course," I continued, "but surely there is something more, out there, over the crest of the mountain or beyond the railroad tracks?"

Walter looked at the full moon as it broke through the trees over our heads and said, "Why go to the unknown when all I need is here? This land remembers me."

It was an intriguing response, one I sort of understood.

Walter seemed to be thinking, perhaps about something that lay beyond words—words that could be shared between a man and a bear, I mean, until he said, "The sky has always watched me here. The winds that blow through these hills... they're like old friends who know every secret, every joy, every loss. If I go somewhere else, it'll be like... losing my name."

One night, late in the season, as the countryside was

beginning to chill, our conversation turned to me when he asked, "Why do you have trouble sleeping?"

I stammered, not quite sure how to respond. Our late night chats over the months had ranged from the mundane to bordering on the esoteric but I was still taken aback.

"Perhaps it's because so much is going on in the middle of the night," I said, "and if I am asleep I might miss something." To deflect the conversation away from me I added, "I would have missed meeting you, for example."

To this, Walter looked at me, his dark features angled up, searching my face. I saw his brow furrow and his eyes focus somewhere in the middle distance between my nose and the back of my head, waiting for more.

"I would," I finally offered, "But the stories in my head keep me awake, or rather, wake me up at night."

He seemed to be taking in my words as he sipped. I glanced at my list of questions attempting to find something to divert the conversation, again away from *me*, until he interrupted—

"Do you find something in the stories that make you a better person?"

I had to think about this, remembering the shelf of novels bearing my name. I searched the characters in them, the insights revealed to me in the moments of writing now spanning more than half my life.

I thought of raising my children, now grown and on their own, and how I worried about them through childhood. How, like the stories, they taught me as much or more as I taught them. And how my smile, though tested during their adolescence, remained as they graduated from university and started a life of their own.

Then, to my wife and the comfort we have been to each

other from our younger days until now, sometime in middle age. While not perfect, in all, the good far outpaced the bad.

"Yes, I think so," I said, "writing helps me better understand who I am, how I see the world."

As he nodded I could see that Walter understood this idea. A thought occurred to me, an outlandish, wild thought that I could never have dreamt for one of my stories: this bear and I were friends.

It was then that I remembered the carving from the night after our first meeting, the tableau of he and I having tea. Even now, months later, I see it often—though my eyes sometimes skim past it on the kitchen wall. And I wondered if more bears, like Walter, have an inner soul, a creative sprite that lives inside them, too?

"Do other bears create? I mean, do they make things?" I ask.

"Yes, sometimes," He said and held up his giant paws to me, "Even these blunt tools are capable of creating when the moon is more full."

Though I wasn't sure he would understand the gesture, I widened my eyes and sipped my tea without saying anything, hoping he would take the opportunity to expound without me leading him to a further answer.

"Seth, all creatures create, not just humans," he said almost matter-of-factly. It was so simple a thought I am embarrassed to note that it hadn't occurred to me.

But Walter didn't stop there.

His great arms spread wide as if gathering all of the night around us and turned toward me to explain, "In spring, wildflowers bloom louder than an orchestra fanfare. The jays that nest just beyond your property are excellent poets. Brown squirrels, climbing up and down collecting acorns, make us laugh by telling jokes. Mighty ant kingdoms are built right below your feet. And the insects, the elders of the forest, the crickets and beetles you hear each night, are constantly whispering stories full of imagination and insight. It's their voices, I suspect, that wake you and also lull you to sleep."

Walter paused, making sure he and I were looking directly at one another as he finished by saying, "Creating is learning, it's what keeps us alive, isn't it?"

I nodded, not wanting to break the spell of his words and the night.

Walter shook, his fur wriggling from his head down to his back. He then rolled his head like he was stretching his neck, much the same as I do after sitting at my writing desk for a number of hours.

"Thank you again for the tea," Walter said. He glanced at the moon, the last of the waning gibbous slipping away, "See you in a few weeks."

When he had gone, I sat in silence and listened to the sound of insects playing, conversing, laughing all around me. I heard harmonies in the skittering and chirping and more as my ears became attuned in the cool night air.

Walter was right, all the world's magic was now available.

At least, for the next few hours.

———

Music to read by:
Concerto for Clarinet and String Orchestra - Aaron Copeland

A HELPING HAND

Mrs. Pillsbury was not at all well.

A regular bout of the sniffles or a summer fever—like the one she had now—might weaken her for a few days, but such maladies could easily be managed with a nip of brandy before bedtime. The strange hand—the extra one—that caught her mid-faint and entirely by surprise was something else, though.

Steadying her, Mrs. Pillsbury forgot all about fainting for a moment as she blinked, staring at the strong, delicate fingers gripping the wooden towel rack of her modest bathroom. Grateful not to have met the tile up close—it was unforgivingly hard—she turned to offer a whisper of thanks, but no one was there.

Looking again at the fingers, her eyes followed the line of the wrist and forearm down, only to discover that the arm terminated—or, more accurately, emanated—from her own stomach.

At this, she was overwhelmed by the sight and, owing to her poor health, lost consciousness. In those darkening fractions of a second before she passed out, a name floated to mind: *Lottie Carmichael.*

————

A few days earlier, the display table at the outdoor market was in shambles. Mrs. Pillsbury huffed under her breath as she attempted, and failed, to corral the topiary guild's show-cased items. In the blustery summer rain, Mrs. Ebert's elegantly grazing fawn had toppled and now dangled from the edge of the table as if clinging to a cliffside by its teeth. Mrs. McGuire's immaculate penguin rolled sideways, its once-effortless glide now a wayward missile headed for destinations unknown.

None of the other ladies made any move to help, absorbed instead in seeking shelter from the spitting rain.

Mrs. Pillsbury's own creation—a simple giraffe, plain and unadorned—precariously tottered off the table before snapping its skyward neck. Mrs. Pillsbury did her best to corral them, but she no longer moved with the swiftness she once had. As she was righting the leafy sculptures, gathering them in her soaked arms, Mrs. Pillsbury overheard Mrs. Ebert whisper at how the sudden death of the giraffe might have been "a mercy killing." To this, Mrs. Pillsbury could only reserve a side-eye, which she saved for another time when she wasn't being pelted with rain.

Only Mrs. Carmichael came to her aid, albeit primarily to protect the plumage of her outrageously perfect peacock. Mrs. Pillsbury watched her work, the rain sliding effortlessly off her jacket, her limbs—only a few years younger than Mrs. Pillsbury's—seemingly immune to the usual maladies of their generation. Mrs. Carmichael appeared to always have a spring in her step, a concentration in her gaze, that the others did not.

Instead, the ladies glanced up from beneath their dry perch—tisking at the sky, dabbing at their temples, and tying gentle bows in the scarves draped over their permed hair. Mrs. Pillsbury watched them as her own shoes filled with rainwater.

It wasn't that Mrs. Pillsbury disliked the ladies of the guild, but they were... Mrs. Pillsbury stopped and thought about it for a minute. They were of little help with *anything* but their own clucking at one another for approval. *Hens,* she thought, and left it at that, picking up the giraffe, its neck slack and draped over her arm.

The others didn't so much as glance at her struggling creation. It wasn't as though they expected much from Mrs. Pillsbury's work—her shapes were always "too plain," too simple, or "lacking artistic vision," as Mrs. Engle once put it over tea. A woman whose idea of artistry involved precariously balanced elephants, Mrs. Pillsbury thought, had little ground to judge.

Later, at the cafe, Mrs. Pillsbury thanked Mrs. Carmichael for her help.

"Ramona, I've always liked you and I hope you won't mind me saying that you're getting on in years," Mrs. Carmichael said, adding, "accepting help is nothing to be ashamed of." She smiled faintly, stirring her tea, adding something about modern science. But Mrs. Pillsbury had tuned out—detesting both the sound of her own first name being invoked, which Mrs. Carmichael did with regularity, and a prepositional ending to sentences.

Still, she reasoned, the guild's plants *had* been saved, mostly unscathed, and with some speed. Though Mrs.

Pillsbury couldn't quite reason how, since Mrs. Carmichael, the always perfectly coiffed and implacable Lottie Carmichael, was barely younger than she.

Through pursed lips, Mrs. Pillsbury said, "I manage my affairs just fine–" but stopped short of more words as her body flinched forward in a great *aa-choo*.

"Of course you do, dear," Mrs. Carmichael said as she sipped her tea, lipstick leaving a pink crescent on the cup, "but couldn't we all use an extra hand?" Mrs. Carmichael extended her manicured hand onto the table and pushed forward a lily-white handkerchief, "Let me send around a care package." Mrs. Pillsbury bristled at this. She was not of the same means.

Mister Carmichael, Mrs. Pillsbury overheard, made a "whopper of a fortune" investing in various companies—ones she couldn't be bothered to remember what they did, or their incredibly silly names. The Carmichaels lived in a large, well-to-do estate with gardeners and the like. If there were any doubt about their wealth, the guild's remaining topiaries, now stowed away in the trunk of their spotless, yellow Cadillac, surely settled the matter.

And if she knew one thing about Lottie Carmichael, it was that "no" was never an answer she would accept.

As Mrs. Pillsbury unpacked the parcel, she found a small tin with a hand-written label: *Thumbs Up Soup—Carmichael's Kitchen Essentials*, alongside a packet of biscuits. Too tired to refuse the gesture, she warmed the soup on the stove. There was a faintly herbal flavor she couldn't place—likely some modern addition—but it was soothing enough that she finished the bowl and thought no more of it as she fell asleep in her most comfortable chair.

Some hours later, she awoke, her neck sore and body

woozy. Before taking her feverish body to bed, Mrs. Pillsbury visited the bathroom. It was there, where the pink hue of the tile reflected on her face and onto the arm holding her aloft.

———

Later, unsure how much time had elapsed, Mrs. Pillsbury found herself in her own bed, duvet tucked gently under her chin. She moved a hand gently under the blanket, hoping, perhaps praying, to find nothing but her squishy midsection. Instead, she found her other hand was being held, cupped gently by this new one—its warm thumb stroking the back of her hand.

Over the next few hours, dozing on and off, soothed, she finally decided the bed was not at all the place she wanted to greet a stranger. Mrs. Pillsbury stood, turning in a circle, looking left then right, but there was no hand. Patting her stomach also revealed nothing, leaving her quite vexed. But as she pulled a heavy pitcher of water from the refrigerator, the hand returned, holding a glass steady as she poured.

"Hmm... a helping hand," Mrs. Pillsbury remarked, recalling Mrs. Carmichael's words, as the hand set the glass gently on the counter and formed a fist, its thumb turned up. She nodded, understanding the gesture of agreement as the hand disappeared again beneath her gown.

And so it went on like this for some time, the hand making an appearance when needed and disappearing again when not. It alerted her when the mail came through the slot in the door, or pointing emphatically at the stove when the water was near boiling. It–she hadn't quite reasoned if the hand was male or female, was equally as proficient at more precise things like chopping vegetables or maneuvering the vacuum. On the whole she found it quite useful, even liberating—if its origin perplexing and the sight of it, perhaps, ghastly.

Other things left her guessing, though. Like when she noticed a stray package of cookies in her shopping cart. Or when Mrs. Grabel's wallet was found in the pocket of her raincoat. Those things, she reasoned, could be simple mistakes. The wallet looked like her own and, well, she'd sworn off those cookies some time ago but they *were* her favorite. All the same, she kept the hand, *it*, out of sight.

———

"Two weeks, ladies!" Mrs. Carmichael said to the assembly of women, her voice echoing in the sitting room of their spacious home, "This exhibit requires your best work. We'll make space available to each of you..."

A cloud of smugness draped over the women as they tittered to one another.

Mrs. McGuire whispered as she motioned toward Mrs. Pillsbury, "Or outside by the trash can." Heads dipped to stifle laughter. Mrs. Grabel smirked–quickly turning it to a mock-frown when she saw Mrs. Pillsbury listening.

That's fine, Mrs. Pillsbury thought, she already knew Mrs. Grabel's opinion: her sculptures were "fine for back-yard hedges, but hardly worthy of display." Others nodded along—polite smiles, gentle tilts of the head—as if Mrs. Pillsbury's efforts were something to be forgiven rather than appreciated.

Only two women of the guild seemed otherwise too occupied to titter: Mrs. Engle, who discreetly tipped another dollop of whiskey into her tea; and Mrs. Rutana, who was busy devouring a plate of petits fours.

Sitting in the back, as she always did, Mrs. Pillsbury watched. Her pencil hovered for a moment, then pressed firmly to the page underlining: grand prize. Of course she'd neither created anything *grand* nor won a *prize* for any effort. But was she not a soul without ideas? Of course she was. And she did have grand ideas. Manifesting them, however, could be tricky. Mrs. Carmichael was right, she was *getting on in years.*

She tapped the notepad then absently began to sketch a shape. Curves of a childish nature formed what might be a dolphin, its mouth open in a most unrealistic way like a pursed kiss. Mrs. Pillsbury scratched it out and started on another. Hand reached out, tapping the paper. Mrs. Pillsbury looked down, then back at the other women who paid her no mind. Hand opened its palm then put its thumb and index finger together, wiggling them at the tip: *Can I draw?*

Mrs. Pillsbury set the pencil in the palm. A quick check of the paper's edge with another finger, Hand turned the pencil over erasing Mrs. Pillsbury's drawing. It wiped the sheet clean of eraser rubber and set to creating a fine shape. Mrs. Pillsbury's eyes widened as she saw the outline, then the details came into focus with each stroke.

Mrs. Pillsbury watched, whispering, "What if…" and pointing at the drawing, her finger moving up then a swift curve down. Hand's thumb went up in agreement as it erased and readjusted the shape.

After a few minutes, Hand paused, the wrist brushing extra graphite from the drawing: *Something like this?*

Mrs. Pillsbury gasped, "Yes!"

One afternoon some weeks earlier, sitting quietly in her garden and enjoying the scents of the gooseberry bushes and sage growing so verdantly, she began to wonder: might she inquire about the hand's intent? From her perspective, it had been mostly a one-way relationship—but she wondered if, too, the hand needed something of her.

"Hand..." she said aloud, not quite sure what to call it, "are you there?"

It suddenly emerged, giving a slight wave before angling to hold her glass of lemonade. This caught her off guard—its willingness to help without being asked.

"I'll hold the glass, thank you," Mrs. Pillsbury said, apologetically.

The hand gave a thumbs up, then began to retreat back to the folds of her blouse.

"Please... don't go. I have a question for you." The hand emerged fully again and turned, palm up, as if to say, *Yes?* It occurred to Mrs. Pillsbury that hand gestures might be an imprecise way to communicate, so she asked if the hand could write if given paper and a pen. It responded with a thumbs up.

On the kitchen table, she set out a pen and a legal pad she found under the pile of mail in her makeshift office. The hand reached out, touching the edges of the pad to judge its size, Mrs. Pillsbury assumed, then felt around for the pen. Like a stenographer, the hand clicked the pen several times, scribbling at an edge to warm the ink, poised to write something. Though she thought quite a lot about the big questions to ask, she had never come around to how she might start the conversation. Mrs. Pillsbury and the hand sat quietly for quite a long moment, her own fingers tugging at her bottom lip, indecisive.

Mrs. Pillsbury thought about how children relate to one another and decided to ask something simpler: "Do you have a favorite color?"

Hand, she, Mrs. Pillsbury had decided since they were from the same body it was a *she*, hovered a moment. It seemed to sway a bit side-to-side before writing: *What color do you like?*

Mrs. Pillsbury huffed. This was not at all what she had expected, a question answered with a question. How rude. Then she considered the hand again, watching her finger tap against the side of the paper, stroking the corner, and it dawned on her: *she had no eyes.*

"Oh..." Mrs. Pillsbury paused to look out the window at the garden, "I like the color green. It's a gardener's color. Calm. Full of life."

The hand perked up, one finger skyward, then wrote: *Green it is.*

Mrs. Pillsbury reflected on this. Colors were a good start but she still knew nothing more than when she had started. She decided the best course was to ask the impertinent: "You seem... young?"

The hand's fingers pinched at the paper corner finding its margin again, and began to write. Mrs. Pillsbury read it aloud as the words appeared, in excellent penmanship: *We are the same age.*

Mrs. Pillsbury's brow tightened a bit as she thought, turning her own spotty and wrinkled hands for another review, though she'd seen them every day for nearly eighty years.

"I find that hard to believe, but–" Mrs. Pillsbury stopped

herself as the hand continued to write. Again, she found herself saying the words out loud: *I - am - you.*

———

The Carmichael estate was expertly decorated for the affair of the season. Partygoers in their summer linen strolled the grounds as servers in black waistcoats moved through the throng like dancing chess pieces. Mrs. Pillsbury clung tightly to her shouldered handbag as she made her way through the foyer and toward the veranda. Below, the garden was seemingly more full of people. There she saw the women of the guild, standing together circled by their draped creations.

Mrs. Pillsbury noted how voluminous some of them were—wider than two men standing shoulder to shoulder, and taller as well. She wondered what might be under each, no expense spared, of course, as they wrought whatever creation to life in laurel and arborvitae. She, too, had experimented with several of those species, though her own creation was seemingly smaller in scale and used mainly the cheaper boxwood varieties.

Mrs. Pillsbury ran a few fingers over the cloth that covered her sculpture. Surreptitiously, Hand, too, reached out to tighten the cover. *All set,* they agreed.

The women of the guild tittered in their circle at one another, voices and cackles shrill among the crowd. As Mrs. Pillsbury approached, some voices turned to a whisper. Heavily made-up eyes, bronzer on their faces, and summer permanents angled toward her in a synchronized pattern, then quickly back to the nattering huddle. *Hens*, Mrs. Pillsbury thought again as she approached, her smile as petite as her frame.

———

Mrs. Pillsbury had never worked with some of the materials Hand pointed out in the hardware store. A couple of clerks helped load the goods into the trunk and back seat of her car. One boy, overwhelmed by the amount and weight, was soon sweating profusely. When Hand appeared and offered him a handkerchief, he didn't seem to notice—but accepted it gratefully all the same.

Packages began arriving daily—boxes of all shapes and sizes—until her patio was littered with cardboard. No matter, she thought, it'll make suitable mulch for the garden if she didn't start a fire while learning how to weld first.

And, at that, she didn't think twice since Hand was so adept at so many things. She merely moved pieces around and held welding goggles to her own face while Hand did her thing in exacting detail.

How Hand knew such things was beyond Mrs. Pillsbury.

———

Mr. Carmichael stood on a decorative pedestal above the crowd as everyone gathered in the garden. Faces watched expectantly as he held his glass aloft and looked from his wife to the group, "Thank you all for coming! I hope you've enjoyed yourself..."

Mrs. Engle tottered, arms crossed, holding her drink close to her lips while Mrs. McGuire scanned the crowd. The others in the guild, too, had one eye on Mr. Carmichael and the other looking at the whos-who of the audience. Mrs. Pillsbury kept herself in the back as usual. She was older than most, perhaps, but not deaf and could hear his booming voice just fine from a distance.

When it came time for the unveiling of the art—*just cleverly shaped bushes*, Mrs. Pillsbury thought—Mrs. Carmichael positioned herself for the best photo opportunity. By her side a member of the guild would pull the cloth away. With a flourish each woman did so, a photographer capturing the reveal in quick flashes, as the audience clapped.

Mrs. Pillsbury watched each reveal one-by-one, all very dramatic and spectacularly bedazzled and adorned.

A trio of victorian Christmas carolers with Spanish moss as falling snow from Mrs. McGuire. Then came the aquatic wonderland of dolphins, also in triplicate, with silver maple leaves as sprinkles of water from Mrs. Ebert.

Mrs. Engle nearly threw herself to the ground unveiling an oversized martini glass with a silver hydrangea onion. The club sandwich from Mrs. Rutana was intricately layered with red coleus as tomato and lambs ear for the lettuce—of course it had a pickle on the top made chiefly of juniper.

Mrs. Pillsbury watched all this from her back row perch. The over-the-top designs were laid out exactly as she and Hand had thought. Their size and construction were, too, each reaching some eight or ten feet in height.

Perfect, she thought. Hand agreed, giving a quick thumbs-up peeking out from the inside of Mrs. Pillsbury's handbag.

———

Mrs. Pillsbury looked again at the words on the paper: *I - am - you.*

Then Hand continued to write as Mrs. Pillsbury watched: *I feel what you feel.*

Her aged eyes had to take another look. Blinking, she

put on her readers, leaning back to make sure the paper was in focus.

Feel? Almost immediately Hand wrote: *Yes.*

Mrs. Pillsbury was unsure how to react. Her face felt flush at the thought of something else knowing her feelings. Was it unsettling? She supposed it should have been. But, no, she didn't feel that way. This helping hand felt like something else. It felt... empowering.

Mrs. Pillsbury began to wonder if Mrs. Carmichael knew all of this? Wasn't she the source of the *Thumbs Up* soup that caused this to happen? But of course, Mrs. Pillsbury thought–Lottie Carmichael must have known this is *exactly* what would happen. Devilishly clever of her, wasn't it? To give the older guild member a helping hand, *this* helping hand.

Mrs. Pillsbury looked to the hand for its thoughts and found it had already scribbled another note on the paper and was pointing: *Tea is ready!*

Steam rose in twisting spirals from the cup as Mrs. Pillsbury sipped, considering her new appendage and what they could do together.

Five glorious and manicured topiary circled the garden courtyard, each more impressive than the one before. They towered over the audience as the guild *ooh'd* for each other in mock excitement.

The last, Mrs. Pillsbury's, sat covered as Mrs. Carmichael walked the length of the grass to its base. Through the crowd Mrs. Pillsbury strode, her stomach in a knot with anticipation. *These last few weeks have been quite the journey,* she thought as she patted the side of the handbag. Her new friend, Hand, had changed everything, had given her a new lease on life and, maybe, a winning design, the *Grand Prize*. And after the ceremony, Mrs. Pillsbury thought, she would like to thank Mrs. Carmichael. The image made her smile: Hand reaching out to shake Mrs. Carmichael's own. She couldn't hide the joy of her, and Hand's, creation.

"Our final entrant is from Ramona Pillsbury…" the audience applauded as Mrs. Carmichael read from a card, "Her piece is entitled 'A Helping Hand.'" Mrs. Pillsbury looked to the audience and gave the widest smile any in the guild had seen. Mrs. McGuire sneered, whispering to Mrs. Grabel.

With a flourish that belied her age, Mrs. Pillsbury pulled down the drape. As it fluttered to the ground the crowd ooh'd as the afternoon light revealed a woman's delicate hand made expertly of twisted boxwood with pale green nails rendered in ornamental kale. And inside the hand set a similarly-sized set of pruning shears fashioned of polished metal. The crowd clapped loudly at the fine detail of each finger, the perceived weight of the overall sculpture.

"Remarkable…" Mrs. Carmichael said aloud.

Mrs. Pillsbury took a breath, savoring the moment. The applause, the admiration, the gaping mouths of the guild— it did feel refreshing, exhilarating, just as Hand told her it would.

Then, she reached down and pulled the lever.

The fingers stirred, then slowly bloomed open—a delicate, deliberate motion, as if the hand itself were stretching awake. The crowd leaned in, marveling. Someone clapped.

Then the shears snapped shut with a metallic clap.

A hush fell over the garden.

The crowd moved forward to take a closer look as Mrs. Pillsbury stepped in front of her sculpture, holding her own hand out to stop them. Another motor inside, wound up tightly, began to inch its gears forward. As the crowd paused fascinated, the gigantic hand turned, shears becoming level with the ground. Then, the sculpture shifted with a loud creak. Mrs. Pillsbury's creation began to roll, massive shears moving faster–open, closed, open, closed. It was closing the distance to the next of the guild's topiary.

Cream filling from an eclair in Mrs. Rutana's mouth squeezed out the other end and onto her blouse. Mrs. Engel's drink tipped forward, the contents spilling over the edge as she laughed aloud in a wild cackle. Mrs. Grabel and Mrs. McGuire stood wide-eyed as they watched the giant hand trundle forward, gaining speed. *Open, closed.*

Shouts from the onlookers screamed, "Watch out!"

Open, closed.

One by one, the guild's work was shredded by the hand and its massive shears. Carolers were decapitated, their songbooks flung into the garden like desperate confetti. The martini glass was cut in half, sending its tragically perfect silver hydrangea olive rolling across the lawn toward a guest's feet. The sandwich, once a masterpiece, was now a crime scene of lettuce carnage and severed tomato rounds.

The dolphins lasted the longest—toppling in slow, majestic despair, heads and fins thrown into the koi pond before sinking beneath the surface.

Onward the hand rolled, shears snipping at the edge of the garden, partygoers scrambling for high ground. Off the terrace, the hand tumbled into the lower garden, still opening and closing like a blinking eye—until, at last, the sculpture tore itself apart, springs and gears flying, boxwood and metal scattering in every direction.

The partygoers remained frozen, staring at the wreckage below—a landscape of torn greenery, broken metal, and traumatized topiaries. Someone sobbed. Someone else cheered.

Mrs. Pillsbury simply adjusted her handbag.

She looked down. From within, her own hand emerged, fingers flexing once before settling into a small but decisive thumbs-up.

Mrs. Pillsbury smiled, mirroring the gesture.

———

Music to read by:
Sibelius: Violin Concerto in D Minor, Op. 47: I. Allegro Moderato

5 DIAS

WITHOUT SEEING IT, HE KNOWS THE HAND IS SHATTERED. Beneath the skin, it's a spiderweb of broken glass.

¡Pinche avispas!

Who knows if that hand will ever again hold a cerveza, a mujer, a fistful of cash.

Right, the money.

Maybe that could fix it. Except he didn't have the money. Not yet.

He remembered watching the brightly lit embers float away at the campsite, carried away by the ocean breeze. Scorching days working the horses and cleaning stables were traded for an afternoon swim, supper and a spot to sleep.

The ranch was hers but not the horses, beautiful and expensive. They were part of a different story, one she rarely mentioned–a gift that came with strings attached.

He caught her looking at him sometimes, her smile warming as she grew fond of his company. And sometimes, a shared bed in her house, long after dark, only when she invited him. Her signal: an open window he could see from his camp. As promised, he'd vanish before dawn, returning to the dying embers of his fire. But he grew accustomed to her scent, her warmth.

That wasn't part of the plan but it sure as hell was now.

He knew to expect the man, the one with the snakeskin boots–*el Jefé*.

"They'll have metal tips. They all do," the woman had told him.

He heard it clear enough and nodded—but *mañana* became a habit, and time slithered off quietly in that *paraíso*. Instead of a last swig of mescal, he remembers a black Mercedes and a hammer. It was the rusted ball-peen from his own toolbox, and a gloved hand swinging it.

As he awoke in the sweltering trunk, he conjured the voice of a baseball announcer: *"Bases loaded..."* the voice boomed. *"Can the rookie Southpaw deliver under pressure?"*

This padded hotbox was as close to the majors as he'd ever get. He knew—if anybody did—he was a rental, a player with a pretty face and a strong back for carrying someone else's grudge.

The other one–the gordito–held him down so the man could do his work. Even by the light of the dying fire the Southpaw saw the circular grains of wood in the stump below his hand. Grooves in a record. He remembers thinking the music skipped when the hammer made contact, before he screamed himself to sleep.

Now, in the suffocating darkness, the announcer's voice echoed in his mind once more: *"Run!"*

But he didn't.

He stared at the faintly glowing handle of the release latch. Just a few more miles, he thought, and then...

———

Northbound on the topside of the Arizona border, sky as far as the eye can see.

This isn't the picturesque valleys of the high desert but flat dirt. It's where a rag of wild colts might dot the terrain, and where coyotes fight for scraps of a spring rabbit. It's Nowheresville at the edge of the Navajo Nation.

On the radio, *Blood, Sweat & Tears* tells us some truth at full volume:

> *What goes up must come down*
> *Spinning wheel gotta go round*

Victor's boot taps the floorboard. His cigarette ash dances along the edge of the window. It's a bad habit he likes. Black coffee and a cigarette makes the mud run. He smiles as the scenery flies by; it's a fine day. There's nothing to be seen for miles, but he keeps checking the rearview.

The passenger, a round-bellied Chingón picked up a dozen years ago, was edgy. His stash was low, and he was due for another bump. He popped pills like a kid eating... whatever the fuck kids eat. Later, Chingón would get his fix, but Victor had to play wet nurse until then. His partner's habit did have advantages; it meant they could roll all night without stopping.

"Stop adjusting the mirror," Victor says.

Chingón puts it back. His head whips back and forth to Victor, looking for approval—a junkie twitch he's recently developed.

"You hear something?" Chingón says, yelling to the open window.

In the wind, the sound of his voice becomes thinner as it rushes back the length of the car, wisping over the trunk as it mixes into nothing.

Victor checks the mirror again.

He's the one you want in control, not Chingón. No vices except the ones we've already discussed. He's sober, married, and, barring any issues with his affinity for 70s yacht rock, exactly the guy you call if there's a problem looking for a solution.

Ya got no money and ya got no home
　　Spinning wheel all alone

Smacking the wheel, Victor's hands keep time with the music. A moon ago, he'd swung a hammer, his favorite tool he never needed to carry. In every town, gas station, and toolbox, there's always a hammer.

Being good at torture doesn't come easy, but it needn't be expensive either.

It made him smile–not the hammer, the swing. Victor thought of it as a love tap, the right sort of thing to bring a man in line.

Ordinarily, Victor liked to swing at a foot—a hobbled patita made it easy for Chingón. But if he chose the hand, it was with a special purpose, a message hard to forget in bones that would never heal in the right way. And true to his exacting nature, Victor always chose the dominant hand.

Victor and Chingón stood in the moonlight, as they had countless times, staring at a poor sack of shit. His usual work of sorting out cartel grudges sucked, but money was money, and Victor had a reasonable, flat rate. This time, though, it wasn't about the payday. This pendejo Southpaw was personal.

Victor picked up the kid, the one from his own hometown, living it up on her hippy farm south of Puerto Vallarta. Victor wondered, *did he know whose mistress he was fucking?*

But Victor couldn't kill him—that's bad voodoo in your own town, like shitting where you eat. No, he'd drop him in the dirty crossroads at home as an example. People had to understand the cost of stepping out of bounds.

> *Drop all your troubles by the riverside*
> *Catch a painted pony on the spinning wheel ride*

The Mercedes hits a bump, sending waves of pain up Southpaw's arm. The grinding of bones was unsettling. His ribs are bruised, too. He didn't remember that part. Without light, he doesn't know exactly how long he's been here. A day, maybe? If so, that makes two days from the coast.

He rolls onto his back, shaking the life back into his good hand, the way a switch-hitter might flex both wrists before stepping into the batter's box.

He hears something and stops. In the car are voices with music playing over them. One of them is the same voice he remembers walking up the gravel road, the one with the metal-tipped boots.

The farm was simple, but it was a cielo compared to the dirt city where he'd grown up, where *los jefes* ran the show. He followed the map south and west along the coast, until he found this place, her hidden Eden. She'd made him the offer of a few chores in exchange for meals and all the open sky he wanted. He couldn't help being taken in by the surroundings – the cliffside villa, the garden with tropical fruit, and hidden playas below for swimming or just staring out at the pacific.

All his life he heard people curse the sky as the sun rose, their workday beginning, while they prayed for night to fall, to finally rest. Their words felt peasant-simple because it wasn't the sky they cursed, it was their life.

Out here, the sun's path across the land changed him, waking him from that shared but forgettable future. But even as he waited, she, too, changed him. Where he once might have seen only toil he began to see a life he couldn't easily forget. Knowing the jefe would soon come, Southpaw watched the sun inch toward the water in a calm orange, before plummeting, furiously blood-red, behind the waves.

He held that image and the shape of her face in mind as the man with the swagger and snakeskin boots appeared at the edge of the property. Southpaw saw him clearly as the polished metal "V" of his boot stubbed out a cigarette in the dirt.

The man held up his palm.

"I'm lost. Thought you might help me."

The man didn't move, but Southpaw could see his eyes search from behind mirrored shades. There could be no mistaking him. Tourists, not the kind who made it out this far, ever wear snakeskin boots.

Southpaw put on his most welcoming smile, "Nobody is ever lost here, Amigo."

Pulling hard on the release, the trunk lid flew open. Southpaw is immediately blinded by the daylight. His eyes see an open road to nowhere, unspooling beyond the bumper of the car.

Behind the wheel, Victor spots the black lid in the rearview and slams on the brakes. Smoke plumes from the tires as the anti-lock brakes skip-*p-p* on the asphalt.

A hard brake at that speed generates about ten times normal gravity. This means our fellas in the car weigh about a ton each as the car slides to a stop. That same inertia affects objects in the car: a cigarette pack collapses as it impacts the windshield, Chingón's bulging eyes dislodge a contact lens, a flailing hand smacks the radio knob, and a revolver neatly placed on the back seat disappears.

Physics is a funny bitch that way.

Pianos start playing in stereophonic sound.

Victor stiff-arms the wheel, trying to keep it straight on the road. It's not that there's anything to hit, just reflex.

Chingón swipes at his face, half-blind in one eye.

Victor's door flies open, even while the car slides to a stop. He's out in a sprint toward the trunk.

It's empty.

She musters a smile
  For his nostalgic tale

Victor circles the back of the car, his head on a swivel as he looks across the landscape for anything, everything. He's looking for the jackrabbit of a man they put there 12 hours ago, the man with the hand as good as a sack of wet napkins.

Only to realize
  It never really was

The passenger door bursts open.

Chingón stumbles out, one hand over his face, muttering at full volume—the unintelligible rambling of a junkie. He bobs up and down, looking toward the backseat for his pistol. He can't tell if it's lost or if he's just blind until he spots something and begins to dig for it.

He frees the gun yelling, "Where'd he—!?"

Victor growls back, "The rabbit hasn't gone far."

Standing in the open doorway, Chingón turns in circles, his arms at full length. His twitchy hands can't hold anything steady in the sights. He's blinking and closing one eye to make the world focus. He's a blob of blind adrenaline and whatever other shit was in his system.

"Amigo!" Southpaw yells.

Chingón turns, instantly pinned by a body slam between the door and car. Both men grunt in pain as Southpaw snatches his gun.

Enough of being rabbit, it's time to be the coyote.

Victor spins toward the noise.

Chingón screams as Southpaw crushes him between the door and frame, half-blind and all stupid.

Southpaw stares Chingón in the face and aims the gun low. The trigger doesn't need to move far. It's a light click— the bullet flows through the air and collides with the top of Chingón's foot, exiting without paying a fare. It stops abruptly in the soft asphalt. The slug, still hot as blood drips on it, sizzles just out of earshot.

What a fool believes he sees
   No wise man has the power to reason away

Both men watch Chingón slide to the ground, wailing in pain.

Around the front of the car, Southpaw moves. He can't leave the man in silver-toed boots with a clear shot. Not the bastard who ripped him from the farm and pinned his hand to a stump like a trophy.

"That is not a nice thing to do to Chingón," Victor says.

Southpaw can't see the man's eyes, but knows he's looking for the next move.

"My ribs disagree," Southpaw yells back.

The air in his lungs is thin; he's panting. Southpaw can feel the throbbing in his mangled hand as he grips the pistol. At best, he's a mediocre shot with his left; who knows how bad he is with the right.

Twenty paces back from the car, Southpaw can hear the man's boots scrape on the asphalt. He wonders, how fast can a man sprint in boots?

"I'd like to talk, are you up for that? Can we be civilized?" Victor says.

The tone has changed. It's almost...friendly?

"I'm not much of a talker," Southpaw says.

Buzzards are nature's perfect garbage disposal. The ones circling overhead have a better view than either of them. Their black eyes look for the easiest meal below and see both men circling the car. The man in boots is further away, slowly cutting back across the road, trying to close the distance.

"It's usually just business. I don't do personal jobs. But you..." Victor says, leaving the implied hanging out there like a dog's tongue on a hot day.

Moving carefully. Slowly.

"Doesn't matter, does it? Here we are. Tell me who your boss is, seguro somos carnales?"

"No boss. Just me," Southpaw says, moving toward the driver's door.

Victor gives a chuckle, "Good to be the boss? Make your own hours, keep all your money."

"Fuckin' A," Southpaw mumbles back, adding, "Your wife, does she know about your girlfriend?"

Victor stops.

A smirk bubbles up on Southpaw's face, "Your wife said you'd eventually come down and check things out. To tell you the truth, I was getting a bit bored."

"You know nothing..." Victor snaps back.

Southpaw winces as he checks his pistol—six rounds. That stupid junkie couldn't even be bothered to fill the clip.

"Very true. She's secretive, your wife. How long have you been gone?"

"Alright, amigo. Enough of civility. Time to feed you to the buzzards," Victor says, the conversation getting the better of him.

Good, Southpaw thinks, *mistakes happen easier when you're rattled.*

"Four? Five days? I figure a stop or two on the way down, maybe another day watching me."

"About that. So?"

"Bueno, cinco es mejor. Yeah. She'll definitely be gone by now."

A shot rings out from Victor's revolver. Southpaw ducks; it's instinctive but the slug only dings the side of the car. It's a message, though to get moving or die.

A boot scrape. Southpaw's head follows it as he says, "You keep a pile of cash around the house?"

Chingón cries an incoherent long vowel somewhere on the other side. He's probably rolling on the ground in the hot sun somewhere below the passenger door.

"She said to mention the emerald pythons. I didn't know what that meant until I saw your boots," Southpaw says.

"How the fu—"

"Ohh…is that where the money is? She says there's probably five million. Half is mine if I keep you away long enough."

Victor's snakeskin boots twist on the asphalt. The metal toe scrapes as he crouches, pivoting toward the trunk.

What seems to be
    Is always better than nothing

Southpaw steps around the driver side of the car. His ears are tuned into everything around him. Here in the middle of nowhere, it's every reptile for itself. The two are rounding opposite sides.

There's nothing at all
    But what a fool believes he sees

There's nothing in Southpaw's vision to shoot. He looks through the car's rear glass and sees it—between the gap in the trunk lid—the other man moving. Victor is still wide of the car and creeping toward the passenger side. Southpaw licks his lips in the hot sun. Each of them at a stalemate until one makes a move. Even the light wind has paused to watch.

Southpaw looks into the car, he's taking inventory— *phone—pill bottle—keys—hamburger wrappers.*

"Oh, you should know we sold the horses. And, your girlfriend..."

He prays for the seconds to do it.

That's all he's got.

"...she says tienes el pene chiquito."

Southpaw drops to the ground using his mangled hand to stop. Every bone collapses in a crunch of potato chips. The splinters of what's left poke through the surface. On the ground, he sights a crouching Victor and fires.

The bullets from his secondary right hand are wild. They're just the fireworks he needs to scare the kids. They're the BOO in the horror movie. They ricochet off the ground as Victor stands, backpedaling for the edge of the road.

Southpaw moves like a rattlesnake backed into a corner, self-preservation veiled as fury. He is in the driver's seat and hits the keyless start.

The engine roars to life.

Victor's boots slip as he tries to make a running start toward the Mercedes.

His gun is out front, leaping to grab anything with a bullet.

What seems to be
Is always better than nothing
There's nothing at all
But what a fool believes he sees

The Mercedes is accelerating at full tilt.

Mach schnell, puta!

Southpaw watches the scene in the rearview mirror shrink until the man in the boots, Jefé, was no longer even an angry dot—he simply ceased to exist.

The sun inched lower, staying a calm orange that never needed to turn furious and blood-red again. It was a new sky, one unburdened by his past.

Her scent drifted on the wind, a reminder of fresh beginnings and untold possibilities.

He took a deep breath, savoring the moment.

Now, it was a fine day.

———

Music to read by:

Stabat Master by Guadalupe Plata

Spinning Wheel by Blood, Sweat & Tears

What A Fool Believes by The Doobie Brothers

En Mi Tumba by Guadalupe Plata

THE WEIGHT OF SNOW

She wanted to see her home as more than severe and unforgiving. That's how it settled in her mind: unforgiving. Standing at the snowy edge of the forest with the frozen lake stretching out before her, the word lingered.

Perhaps a poet—one hardened enough to make it out this far—might have described it in more picturesque terms. But she wasn't a poet, and for her, it was those things—a place she wished she could imagine as softer, kinder, but...

She moved forward, her eyes on the distance, where the snow gathered heavier against the far bank. There was a place she needed to see, a place waiting under all this weight.

"He always called me Queen Anne," she thought. "I could've hit him with a brick every time it came out of his filthy mouth."

She sees herself with the brick, the loose one from the hearth, the corner one that always gets kicked to the floor. Heavy in her palm, she feels it and sees herself moving it back into place.

The images of the brick fade as flecks of snow sweep her

eyelashes like crystalline razors. The hood of the old jacket flapped as she glanced ahead, squinting.

"And here I am dragging my tired ass out to see him," she said to herself, the words whisked away.

Footsteps, slow and steady, rose over one snowdrift after another and back down. Even on snowshoes, her body sank deeply in the white until the last rise sloped slowly downward toward the massive lake with mountains all around.

"I showed him how to cross the lake in winter, snow up to our armpits," she laughed. "Showed him everything. The fool... before me he never chopped wood, never caulked a bath."

She stood, huffing, big billows of vapor rising from the dark hood against the white.

With one hand she followed a toppled tree, roots frozen in place like a silent scream. Her hand slid along its long trunk, steadying herself as it sloped down, disappearing into the ice.

"But he had a charm. One that'd rub off on you from time to time."

Pulling down her scarf, she let her tongue out, catching snow. She let her head stay uncovered that way for a long moment before running the back of her gloved hand across her mouth.

On the ridge beyond, she saw a stroke of black and watched the slowly moving shape. They were both going the same direction. She knew this shape, knew its shoulders, the lumber of its steps, the brow tines and the points that led up and away, filling out the heavy, bony rack.

He had called it Bullwinkle. Said it with a laugh every time. He even tried to feed it, make friends with it.

"Out paying your respects?" she said to the moose. It

snorted as it sniffed down low. It wasn't responding to her or anything but its own stomach.

Her eyes followed it as her steps slowed, listening. Far away was the wind, topping the trees and loosening the lightest snow on their shoulders. Further, there was nothing —maybe just a skitter of snow on the ice. Below her feet, the snow gathered in winding clumps like shifted sands, a pattern made by whim.

Snow is random, not orderly, she thought. It can come down from above and sideways at the same time. The wind lifts it off the bank, mixing with the flakes still falling, swirls it all up together before throwing it back down.

Like Liar's Dice, she thought. That's what he called it. Five dice in a cup—guess how many of each are face-up, then spill them out. For hours he'd win. She hated it. He always liked the bluffing games: Skulls & Roses or Perudo. Those kinds of games made her blood run.

If not for the snow billowing across the lake, she could retrace her steps from the day before. But it's February, and the daily snow erases footprints as if with a giant eraser. Like him, erased. One day he was sipping tea, the fire crackling and the next he was somewhere else.

Early in the dark, he'd slipped from the sheets and made his way to the wood stove. She didn't remember the sound of the kettle or him stoking the fire. But she heard the clatter of his mug, the chips making a tinkling sound as they scattered. She could hear it in every step on the ice—the slow creaking of the shards, sharp and high-pitched like whispers as her feet pressed lightly, moving forward.

She didn't remember shaving his face except for watching the hair crackling and burning in the stove. A whoosh of energy, a wincing smell. She wondered how many years it had been since she'd seen his unshaven face.

And in that, she thought she might have loved him more honestly had she seen the roundness of his cheeks, the dash cleft on his chin more often. He was there on the floor, then part of him, up the stove pipe and out into the air. On that calm day, the smoke would drape across the valley for hours, the man soaring above the trees. He'd like that.

"This place is too small for your books to be left out," she told him many times. She meant it; the square of the cabin, such as it was, didn't leave much room for not being neat. He was anything but tidy. His books, like his thoughts, were always a mess, always scattered about. A fool, off for some adventure or another in those words. He'd want to tell her about it while she was busy making supper or doing a puzzle. His daydreams drifted so far from the reality of their little cabin that she sometimes wondered if they even shared the same life. Her worries were never his, and she made sure he knew it—her feet always grounded while his were somewhere else.

A howl, echoing across the lake, snapped her back. That sound gave her shivers more than the ice under her feet— the winter wolves, hungry and willing to take a chance on anything. Then another howl, somewhere higher. They were converging, one making its way along the bank, the other angling down from the top of the ridge.

She'd lost track of Bullwinkle, his massive frame hiding from sight behind a tree for a moment before emerging again up ahead. His antlers dipped toward the ground, sifting through the drifts for greenery. Even at this distance, she could see the calm sureness in his steps—steady, deliberate. He knew the way, she thought, just the same as she did.

Wolves didn't come around the cabin much. The last one that tried had met the snap of her shotgun—a spray of rock salt that sent it yelping into the trees. She could still remember the streak of its shadow on the snow, the trembling in her hands as she reloaded, just in case it circled back. They mostly kept their distance now. Bears, too—but bears didn't work in teams.

"Come listen," he had said from outside, the last light dipping behind the hills as the stars woke up. A single yip echoed from a cub on the far shore, followed by a whole litter—maybe five or six of them. Their playful chattering bounced off the water and through the thickened summer trees. She had been cautious, though, putting the shotgun behind the front door, just in case. He could have all the mosquitos and late-night howls he wanted; she had other things to attend to. Something in the house always needed fixing, tidying, or throwing away. Even without kids to tear things up, she was on duty for all the things he had no mind to.

The memory dissolved as her eyes fixed on Bullwinkle's shape. He stood still, his large rack turned, one ear pricked forward. She followed his gaze to where she thought he might be listening. There, some ways off, she saw a gray shape making its way over the snow, its back rising and falling with each leap. She couldn't hear it, but Bullwinkle could. It was bigger than a dog, heavy with fur, and running full-tilt. Strange, she thought, to see one running at such a pace.

She moved her feet faster on the ice, sliding more than stepping, as fast as she dared. Her man might have whooped or whistled to get Bullwinkle's attention, but she knew better than that. A moose could outrun—or at least outfight—a single wolf, but if the wolf turned its attention on her, she'd stand no chance. A person, woman or not, alone on the ice would be torn apart.

That's when she saw the others. Did she see three? Maybe it was four. Black and gray boulders of fur making their way down the rise from the far side behind the moose.

She wasn't close enough to see their eyes, but she knew what they looked like. She knew they'd be narrowing in on the prey, or where the prey would be, somewhere ahead wherever the decoy chased it.

Crackling under her feet, the ice sent notice of her movement. But she knew this area and knew it would hold firm as she moved closer to the bank. She reasoned that you could probably drive a truck over it this time of year. Hers was back at the cabin, nestled under several feet of snow and a heavy tarp to keep the critters from chewing the wiring. Too far to go back in a hurry and not at all useful. She'd continue, carefully. All she could think of was a broken hip—one slip on the ice and down she'd go. Not underneath the ice, but out flat on top of it. She'd freeze, probably before the wolves found her. But they would, eventually.

She watched as the pack came down the slope. One yelped as it lost footing and fell from an embankment, tumbling.

The moose heard this, his legs quickly shifting. She saw it weighing the options, turning in a small circle to gather distances, taking in the scent. In the summer, it could tire them, lead them on a merry chase so long they'd eventually give up. But in the winter, with drifts up to its knees, the wolves would have an easier time catching him.

No, this would be a short chase, and a fight where the odds weren't on the side of the moose.

Under a nearby tree at the bank, she ducked, the decoy wolf racing by just ahead of her. She could smell the wet fur long after the mottled streak had passed through the snow.

Bullwinkle stomped, turning his body toward the beast. With a great flourish of size, his massive antlers swayed back and forth. She could see the hair on his back standing upright.

Shadows from behind grew closer, closing the distance. Every paw scrabbled, every flank stretched to reach what would certainly be a catch to feed the entire horde.

And then Bullwinkle froze, standing as still as the tree she was under. Snow seemed to hang in midair, uncertain about what would happen next. One ear flattened to the oncoming wolf as the other slowly angled to listen in the other direction.

She held her breath as she watched his skin tighten, his front hooves angling down, planting themselves, his body seeming to coil like a snake. A long, slow cloud of steam came from Bullwinkle's nose as his head lowered, leveling itself at the approaching wolf.

From behind, the closest hound jumped. With a quick turn, faster than she'd ever seen a moose move, Bullwinkle twisted his massive body, swinging his rack in the air like a tentacled baseball bat. With a sharp crack, they made contact with the wolf's muzzle and front legs, the full force twisting the wraith sideways. The dog let out a painful yelp and lay in the deep snow, its body writhing and seemingly unable to right itself.

In their tracks, the other dogs slid to a halt. The lead wolf that had darted past her was too far ahead, running too fast to stop as Bullwinkle swung his great head back in another arc. This time, the antlers, twisted and low, caught the streaking wolf in the midsection, its paws scratching the moose's shoulder as it made contact. But the weight of the antlers and a pointed end caught purchase, plunging deep into the wolf's ribs, its body lifting as the moose flicked its mighty head skyward.

Her eyes closed as she heard another scream—a piercing, debilitating howl from the lead wolf as its body was tossed into the snow near the moose. She could see the dog still writhing as the moose stood to full height and raised its front hooves, smashing them down again and again as the mottled gray shape in the snow turned to red. Yowls of pain from the wolf mixed with snorts and grunts from Bullwinkle as he jumped and kicked like a wild bronco being let out of a chute.

At once, it stopped as the moose let out a long bellow, a shout—not the playful trumpet she had heard in the past, but an angry, exhausted bombast of a sound that echoed across the lake.

Stopped in their race down the ridgeline, the other two dogs paused, watching intently. They neither turned away nor ran but stood fixed, observing the scene unfolding below. She watched as the pack, now half its size, seemed to deflate. Unlike humans, who would throw themselves headlong at the emotion of a situation, these scavengers only looked on as their kin moaned and, after a few moments, stopped moving completely.

She had never witnessed such forces collide, their brute, wild logic laid bare. It reminded her of the way something fights to stay alive long after it's broken—the instinct to resist an ending, even when the cracks seem too deep to mend.

Watching Bullwinkle stand his ground, blood streaking his legs and breath clouding the air, she thought of the man —how he'd try to reason with her, to say his piece, even voice his anger, only to meet her sharp words and colder silences. Still, like the moose, he never wavered.

Pawing at the ground, the moose turned in a small circle, looking up the hill. Swinging his head side to side, he looked directly at the two salt-and-pepper hounds. For a long moment, all the animals stood still.

Above them, heavy clouds laden with morning snow descended the mountain in wisps and strands of gray and pearl. The two wolves on higher ground retreated back up the hill—not disappearing entirely, but giving the moose room to move freely.

From beneath the brush, she stepped forward, heavy clumps of snow falling from the disturbed branches above. Bullwinkle startled at the sound of her movement, swinging his massive head toward her.

Holding one hand aloft, she said nothing but stayed motionless. He huffed, vapor curling from his flared nostrils before the wind swept it away.

Could he smell her? Of course, she thought. She was upwind and, glancing at the hood of her coat, she remembered: she was wearing his jacket. Maybe Bullwinkle remembered him, too—the man and the basket of rotting apples he'd left near the cabin. Bullwinkle had eaten them all, along with her handmade basket.

She held steady until the giant moved first. The blood on his legs left deep red stains streaking the snowdrift behind him, vivid against the shadowless white.

She followed, her snowshoes sinking slightly with every step, keeping her distance and one eye on the ridge. Wolves, she knew, for all their pack camaraderie, were opportunists. This time of year, they wouldn't hesitate to return to a fresh kill once it was safe. She knew they'd be waiting just over the ridge, hidden in the clouds.

Following the high edge of the lake was slow going, even on the windward side where the snow swells were thinner. She gulped heaping breaths of air, trying to keep up.

For every two of Bullwinkle's steps, she took five, the pair forming an unlikely remuda. The wind stung her face, her legs heavy as she pushed forward, tightening her jaw to keep the thought of turning back at bay.

She thought of the cabin, now far behind, and of swimming too far from the shore. The man had been a strong swimmer, diving from their little dock and emerging halfway across the lake, never out of breath. She could still hear his laugh, sharp and full of life, echoing through the hills as she stood wrapped in a blanket, unwilling to join him.

"You're an old fool!" she'd shout, dourly and for effect. She knew anything above a whisper carried easily over the still lake. He'd wave a hand, deflecting the words in his usual mild way. But her tone—the sting of it as the words whipped off her tongue—always landed. She remembered doing that a lot: being aggravated at him for doing something his way instead of hers, and saying so, just for spite.

Later, when he'd ask her about it, his hand gently trying to smooth the indelible crease on her forehead, she'd busy herself with something else. Her list of grievances, endless and ever-growing, was a stitch in her side she couldn't let go. She wouldn't let his kindness be a balm.

Their love was a mended patchwork quilt, worn but enduring. He was always comfortable wrapping her in the middle, his body close to hers, even as the tattered edges gave her fits. He'd spill grounds on her countertop, but the coffee was always hot in the morning. She'd see only weeds in the garden, overgrown with everything he'd planted— everything they'd need for the summer and to fill the root cellar for fall.

As Bullwinkle paused just a few feet ahead, she realized she'd reached her destination. She didn't need to look up; she knew the tree's branches by heart. Kneeling, her hand swiped at the flecks of snow covering the tough, wrinkled bark and the patch where his carving would always be.

Her gloved hand traced the letters, the lines deep and jagged, his familiar scrawl etched into the bark. Words had never been her strength, not like they were for poets. If they had been, maybe the kinder words would have come out more often. More forgiving. More like the ones he'd left here just for her.

———

Original music composed by Nolan Green:
The Nature of Winter

Alternate music to read by:
Susy Passes - Michael Giacchino
I See The Sky - Michael Giacchino
Long Ride Home - Patty Griffin

THE ZENO PARADOX

<u>ACT ONE</u>

As the elevator descended, Hanna heard screaming. Already, she could feel the vibration of its warble on her skin as the steel box moved closer. She looked at the buttons on the control panel—Up or Down. Any normal elevator would have an emergency stop switch or a call box. A third option. But here, nothing. Pass or fail.

"Binary," she thought. Just like the system her father had devised—a system built around simple choices, his.

The doors opened, sirens ringing from every corner as lights flashed. She paused, closing her eyes, taking a long deep breath through her nose. Waiting a moment, it came out in one long exhale. She tried like hell not to let it take her breath, but as the sound grew louder, her heart raced.

As Hanna exited the elevator, the brickwork appeared to vibrate, pulsing in rhythm with the emergency lighting. From memory she followed the long corridor leading past the galley, its stainless steel surfaces reflecting the flashing lights. Then a control room, glowing with the light from dozens of screens. The structure, she thought, was unchanged—yet somehow different, lived in.

All paths led to the main room: a library and the portal. In the cacophony she spotted him—Captain McDonnell. He stood rigid and hunched, staring intently at a tablet computer. Still in his uniform, maybe always, his name badge caught the glow of a clock on the wall:

2:50…2:51…

"C'mon, Thompson, make a decision," McDonnell said to the screen on his tablet as if willing something to happen. Hanna hadn't met him in person, but she knew his type—all brass buttons and soulless efficiency. It was his call that had awakened her just yesterday.

McDonnell was courteous, if officious, until the pretense was over, "We need your help."

Wait, was it help he asked for? No, he phrased it differently. McDonnell had said, *"Warren* requested you." Her skin ran cold, her father's name used colloquially for a machine. But McDonnell didn't elaborate further, simply providing transportation details and a schedule that led to now.

McDonnell's words reverberated in her head as she stood there, the lights making caverns of the library. And then she wondered, standing in this carefully manufactured world, whether he—or rather, it, *The Nexus*—had requested Hanna, or *Bunny,* her father's pet name for her, the one he'd use to coax her participation.

02:53…02:53…

Hanna watched the clock. Did it just skip? Maybe she

blinked and missed it, the way a TV sometimes does when you glance away for a moment.

02:54...02:55...

She looked at the room; it hadn't changed much in the twenty-some years since she'd been here. The clock was new, but the portal, the blacked-out round door that led to the simulation chamber, was the same. The library, too, was an extension of her father's penchant for modern simplicity: a tidy seating area flanked by parallel book-shelves holding a relief map of world events rendered in text. Each book a precise transcription of humanity's key events.

Her eyes moved along the stacks, ticking off subjects: Napoleonic Wars, Victory or Retreat, partition of India, the space race. They were reference materials, studied for use in the simulation chamber—scenarios where judgment and consequence had already been rendered.

02:56...02:57...

Another siren, a different one, rang out. The clock stopped, numbers frozen as the lights stopped blinking. In the silence, she heard McDonnell's ape-like breathing in heavy heaves. Still staring at his tablet, he watched the network map—a spider web with one node blinking red, then yellow—finally turned green. A signal that the system could continue.

For all its vast reach as a predictive learning machine, The Nexus still had to wait for a human response. Her father had built it that way, purposefully limiting its capabil-ities. As if tying one hand behind its back or making it stoop

—if for only a few minutes—handicapping the system just enough to force humanity to intervene.

McDonnell exhaled in one final huff as he straightened, seemingly as relieved as the system itself.

"Captain," Hanna said aloud.

McDonnell spun around, surprised. "Dr. Lightman."

She gave a faint smile, the one she reserved for eager students or the lingering guest at a cocktail party who would rather talk about her father than any work she had published. It wasn't unkind, she thought, just the necessary one, the one that kept herself at arm's length.

He seemed relieved to see her, still paying more attention to the tablet than the forced guest. His tablet beeped as the clock reset: *zero.*

The portal spun open as a man, drenched in sweat, fell to the floor. Hanna watched as McDonnell helped him to a seat in the library. McDonnell handed the man a bottle of water as he sat down, his breath rasping. They watched as he drank the entire contents, as though quenching a week-long thirst.

Thompson's hands trembled as he looked at McDonnell. "What was the time?"

"Too damned close. We were almost locked out," McDonnell answered.

Hanna stood, hands neatly clasped in front. She knew this was the way, an affectation for hiding her nervousness.

Waiting for Thompson to regain his composure, she spotted the painting. She didn't have to read the nameplate to know the face: Dr. Warren Lightman. Of course her father's portrait would be hung prominently in the library. The watchful eye of the creator, his gaze focused somewhere off on the horizon, toward the portal. His look in the painting was different from those commissioned for biographies, the ones with a piercing stare, suited for stark black and white dust jacket covers. This one, she thought, was more hopeful, enigmatic. *This* look was for posterity—his subtle way of denoting that he would forever oversee every choice made in the room, tethering them all to his vision.

"I wasn't ready for the rumble," Thompson said, his voice shaking. "My stomach dropped before I was pulled down into the seat. The weight was intense..." He paused, the memory clearly unsettling him. "I could see the patches on their suits."

"A new simulation?" McDonnell asked.

"Yes," Thompson whispered, his voice barely audible. "Onizuka, Resnik... I was beside them."

McDonnell thought for a moment, then his face dropped.

"Jesus, the Challenger..."

Thompson nodded, looking down. "It's scary as hell in that cockpit. As soon as I figured out where I was, I was... afraid for them, and wished there was some way out."

On his tablet McDonnell pulled up a schematic of the STS-51-L Space Shuttle, the Challenger, showing the front seats labeled: Pilot Michael Smith, Commander Francis "Dick" Scobee. Behind them were Ellison Onizuka and Judith Resnik, and the mid-deck held by Ronald McNair, Christa McAuliffe, and Gregory Jarvis.

Thompson cleared his throat. "I would've expected something like... 'Launch or Abort,'" he said, frowning. "This time, there was a single word on the console..."

Thompson pointed to an empty spot where he'd been in the simulation, a phantom seat next to Onizuka, then traced his finger toward the outline of the instrument console.

"It might have been a button, not the normal kind. It was too far to reach. Another anomaly."

"Was anything else out of place?" Hanna asked, stepping a bit closer.

Thompson looked at her for a long moment. Then, his eyes registered recognition before shaking his head, no.

Hanna gave a slight smile and said, "It's good to see you again, Dr. Thompson."

Thompson nodded, still catching his breath.

Hanna studied the man's face, then the schematic on the tablet. After a moment her eyes shifted to the library and its high shelves filled with history books. Each row neatly trimmed up, no book out of place, no detritus like you'd find in a public library except a fine layer of dust.

"It was the failsafe again?" McDonnell asked.

"Yes—twice in a week," Thompson confirmed, looking at Hanna. As Hanna walked, her eyes drifted to the top of the stacks. It was smaller than she remembered, not as imposing. But it was still a replica of his study from their home, the one she remembered, where she'd spent countless hours.

"Bunny," she remembered him saying, *"we're not here to rewrite history. You have three minutes to choose the correct answer before the computer takes over."*

She'd look at the images, searching her memory for the correct answer. Just photographs back then, nothing like what became the simulation chamber. Instead, she'd have a two-dimensional view of a scenario to react, and the clock was always ticking.

Back then, the system had been just a schematic, a logic chart for what would become an expansive AI network. Her father had called it *The Nexus* with the tagline *"a learning computer to help humanity."*

It would quickly grow to include a network of AIs spread across the globe, each tasked with guiding, adjusting, and directing to keep society from straying too far from the optimal path. The Nexus could execute decisions with lightning speed, tirelessly keeping stock markets stable, farmlands yielding, perhaps even halting terrorist threats before they could emerge.

For all its power, the Nexus was ultimately just a machine—a system without conscience. And so, at its heart, deep underground in this bunker, was its most essential component: the human interface, the simulation chamber.

She remembered her father's practiced voice, the conviction in it each time he said, *"History is the lock. To open it, we need someone—a human—to provide the key."*

Her father had insisted on it. A safeguard, a way to keep the system tethered to human judgment. Only a person— someone trained to articulate an historical choice—could keep the Nexus from drifting into cold, calculated efficiency.

"Three minutes never feels like enough, does it?" Hanna murmured, her thoughts drifting toward a distant memory.

"Three minutes," McDonnell answered in a practiced tone, "is the threshold where people freeze, second-guess, or refuse the choices altogether. The system is accounting for, well, stage fright."

Hanna smiled as she rounded the library stacks, looking at the two men. The portrait, she now noticed, had a clear view of the entire room, unencumbered by anything—the watchful eyes, the all-knowing face.

"A three minute timer is... arbitrary," Hanna said. She watched the two men turn their eyes to her. "It's a red herring. My father could have made it any amount of time."

Thompson and McDonnell looked at one another.

"Think about it," Hanna continued, "The Nexus has already made the decision, probably trillions of them, in fact, by the time we decide to push a button."

"So, what's it waiting for?" McDonnell asked.

Hanna took another look at the painting. She was closer now, and the dabs of paint were visible, making the image distorted and abstract. There was something unsettling about seeing the artist's work up close, a way it was never meant to be seen.

A thought struck her. "It's waiting..." Hanna said, "to be right." She realized it was his method—perhaps even his ego—embedded in the system, ensuring every choice passed through his singular logic.

Thompson leaned back slightly, his gaze drifting toward the ceiling as though seeking clarity in the silence. "It didn't give me a choice, though. It just glitched again. In the shuttle with those astronauts, that teacher...felt like there was no right answer."

Hanna watches Thompson closely. Even though the simulation is over, the experience of being in that doomed shuttle has left him visibly unsettled.

"But why the failsafe if it already knows the answer?" McDonnell asked, his tone sharp as he studied the tablet in his hands.

Thompson shrugged slightly and took a deep breath, his chin arcing to his chest as if the floor might offer answers he couldn't. McDonnell tapped the edge of the tablet with his thumb, a rhythmic gesture to occupy his hands while waiting for the others to respond.

Hanna crossed her arms, her voice steady as she wondered aloud, "Maybe it's stuck—caught on something it can't resolve. Like Turing's halting problem or Gödel's incompleteness theorem."

Thompson grunted softly, as if a thought had just clicked, then shrugged. "Zeno's paradox?" he said, his tone carrying the faintest edge of doubt, dismissing it even as he spoke.

McDonnell blinked, shifting his focus. "Zeno's what?" Hanna stepped forward slightly, intrigued by the notion, turning it over in her mind.

Thompson folded his arms across his chest, his posture mimicking Hanna's. "It's an old philosophical idea. Zeno argued that progress happens in smaller and smaller steps—always getting closer, but never actually reaching the end."

McDonnell raised an eyebrow. "Alright, but this is a *machine*. It doesn't 'move'—it calculates."

"It's not just about movement," Hanna interjected, glancing at Thompson before addressing McDonnell. "Zeno used it as a framework to describe both movement *and* math—decisions broken down into a series of steps. Each step gets smaller, closer to the goal, but you never actually reach the goal."

Thompson adds, "Always approaching, but never arriving."

McDonnell gestured to his tablet, skeptical. "It doesn't hesitate. It calculates. So, again, if it knows the answer, why wouldn't it just finish?"

Thompson shrugged, his tone is cautious, scientific. "What if it's doing exactly what it was designed to do—calculating every possible step, narrowing in on every variable—but something is keeping it from making the leap? Something it wasn't built to handle?"

McDonnell frowned, his gaze bouncing between them. "Like what?"

Hanna tilted her head, her gaze drifting to the overhead lights. For a moment, she is distracted by the dust floating in the beams, barely visible until it caught just the right angle.

She exhaled softly. "Zeno's paradox wasn't meant to be solved—it was meant to show how some problems can't be resolved by logic alone. If the Nexus is stuck, it's because it's doing exactly what it's supposed to do: processing, refining, calculating. So, maybe this problem isn't logical."

McDonnell adjusted his tie, his expression guarded. "Are you saying the Nexus is too smart, or not smart enough for its own good?"

Thompson's lips pressed into a thin line."Maybe it's not about being smart. Maybe it's looking for an answer when it doesn't understand the question."

Thompson shakes his empty water bottle then walks over to a cabinet and opens it, his hands still shaking, revealing a few nearly empty bottles of liquor. Hanna noted, wryly, that her father would never have allowed it to sit that empty. Thompson poured a finger of whiskey into a glass and took a sip.

Hanna looked into the empty space between them, the hum of the overhead lights filling the silence.

McDonnell shifts, his body language careful, the mask of someone trying to be in control while clearly out of his depth. "Alright," he said finally, "If it's stuck like you say, maybe that's why you're here?"

Hanna felt a familiar knot tightening in her chest—an echo of the moments her father's work had drawn her into the spotlight. Had she ever truly escaped it, or was this where she was always meant to end up?

Hanna smoothed her shirt and straightened her name badge, buying herself a few more seconds to consider the question. "Is the failsafe a verbal command to stop the simulation?" she asked.

"Yes. If the system encounters a fault and no selection can be made, it displays a keyword to be spoken aloud,"

Thompson said. "I wrote the protocol, but not the keyword. Honestly, I never thought we'd actually use it—it was so long ago."

"What was the failsafe command?" McDonnell asked.

Thompson wiped sweat from his brow, uncurling a finger from his glass, and pointed at her nametag. "Same as last time. It said, *'Hanna.'*"

<u>ACT TWO</u>

Looking more closely, Hanna saw the true age and disrepair of the facility. Dust settled thickly in the corners, scuff marks lined the once-pristine walls. Cracks veined the concrete floor beneath her feet, each fracture a silent testament to years of relentless use—a place built to endure rather than to be cared for.

Hanna wondered if the Nexus itself could register neglect—as if a system built purely on calculation could recognize the difference between mere operation and genuine vitality. The Nexus wasn't built to feel; it was built to endure. And endure it had, for over twenty years.

"It's been a while since you were here?" McDonnell asked as they stood at the intersection of several long corridors.

"Not since I was very young," Hanna said. "It was just a few rooms then. It's changed quite a lot."

McDonnell gestured down the hall. "The barracks were added some time ago. The teams, assigned by *Warre–*, um, The Nexus, have grouped themselves by region."

"How many?"

"When it's full, about sixty," McDonnell replied. "But right now, only Dr. Thompson is here."

Hanna paused, considering the range of simulations that might require so many people. She suspected the staffing followed seasonal patterns—more world-shaking events, after all, seemed to happen from summer to autumn, fewer in winter. It was a rabbit trail, but with June approaching, she expected the roster would be close to full.

"Bunny, pay attention," Dr. Lightman had said, his didactic voice prompting as he pointed to the architectural scale model on his desk. She remembered thinking how

much it looked, parts of it anyway, like his office—clean, modern furniture, reading chairs near the twin bookshelves like those in the library. A model within a model.

"The data server room, simulation chamber, and library come first—their purpose is central," He'd say, *"They're the hub of the system."* She'd listen to him, imagining how being in that space might feel in real life. With its open top allowing a clear view of the details inside, the model never felt claustrophobic—nothing like the real thing.

"Why use your name as the failsafe?" McDonnell asked.

Hanna thought for a long moment before offering, "Old men, clinging to the past, I suppose."

Thompson may have written the protocol, but she knew her father's hand was in it all along—perhaps his way of binding her to this place, a captive audience via the smallest lines of code.

They moved past rooms lined with sturdy, utilitarian furnishings. Hanna glanced into one room, noting sketches on the walls—a waving flag with an eagle clutching thunderbolts, a ringed hand adorned with a bee, and a curved saber inscribed with *"Honneur et Patrie."*

"Honor the Fatherland..." Hanna murmured.

McDonnell nodded. "That phrase gets recycled throughout his tory, doesn't it?"

"Yeah," Hanna said, "I didn't expect it to pop up stateside so recently."

"In a Napoleonic-era simulation," McDonnell continued, "Dr. Maupin said he caught that inscription on a sword just as the guillotine took Desmoulins' head." He paused, adding with a chill, "The choice was *loyalty* or *dissent.*"

She shivered. Simulation or not, it felt too real, the weight of history up close.

McDonnell guided her into the central control room,

where monitors displayed the status of AI nodes worldwide. Satellite imagery highlighted locations across the continents. Hanna spotted a few: cities flaring red with civil unrest, regions where food supplies were running low, and isolated points marked for political instability. She saw Paris, Cairo, Hong Kong—and, unexpectedly, Des Moines.

"Iowa?" she asked, raising an eyebrow.

"Political demonstrations," McDonnell replied, barely looking up. "Sometimes it's small things in unlikely places. The Nexus monitors all of it."

The screens pulsed softly as new markers appeared and vanished in real-time, each point representing a decision or action, each flicker a reminder of the constant vigilance her father's creation demanded.

On the main screen in front of them appeared a timeline as McDonnell swiped on his tablet, controlling the view. Hanna watched the various markers scroll by, each indicating a simulation by the Nexus. Today's simulation of the Challenger explosion was highlighted in red while others were green: *Battle of Thermopylae, The Gunpowder Plot, Cuban Missile Crisis.*

"Okay, so like your father envisioned, the Nexus nodes constantly make decisions in the real world. Most of the time it just does its thing, but every so often it needs approval. Except, the system abstracts the decision with a simulation, a surrogate, to get approval from us."

Hanna thought, *Us.* He means a human.

"Right, the simulations aren't tied to the actual decision, just a key," Hanna said.

"Exactly." He tapped a flashing yellow marker. "About a year ago, things changed."

The marker highlighted: Tribunal of Joan of Arc (1431).

"This was the first anomaly," McDonnell explained. "In the simulation, Joan's trial progressed as expected, but just as her sentencing was announced, an odd detail appeared. On a wooden table near the judge's bench—a single document, printed on modern, perforated paper."

"Dot matrix... in the 15th century?" Hanna asked, frowning.

Thompson entered quietly, adding, "The document contained a single line: 'Undefined error.'"

Hanna's eyes narrowed. "An error in what?"

Thompson's expression tightened. "In the simulation, the choices were *Recant* or *Defy*."

"But Joan chose defiance," Hanna said, puzzled. "Wasn't that outcome clear?"

Thompson nodded slowly. "It should have been. But the moment I tried to touch a button, the system stalled. The execution order froze, caught between advancing and holding her fate in suspension."

Hanna frowned, unsettled. An undefined error, in a system built to predict every outcome? It was as though something was missing—a detail it couldn't place, maybe, or a hesitation. She filed the thought away, her mind catching on the strangeness of it. "Hmm... The Nexus faltered despite a clear decision?"

"Yes," McDonnell replied, uneasy. "Eventually, it played out—but not before that hesitation. And the document."

Thompson reached into his pocket, frowning as he patted his other pockets. "I think I've spotted something... a pattern, maybe. Must've left my notes in the library. Give me a moment."

As he left, McDonnell's eyes followed him, then shifted to Hanna. "He's been on edge with these anomalies. Spends hours rechecking the Nexus logs, sometimes two or three times. Says he's seeing a pattern... but hasn't explained what he means. Maybe you know Thompson better than I do..."

He let the words hang there, perhaps hoping she would fill in the ending. But she couldn't. Hanna turned over what she'd heard, the puzzle still a scattered pile of pieces with no clear edges. An exploding space shuttle, the sentencing of a young woman—a girl, really—with visions.

McDonnell's voice broke her thoughts. "Shall I go on?" She nodded, refocusing on the timeline. The screen flipped forward.

"And then... the Salem Witch Trials simulation. In this case, the simulation placed Martha Corey at the execution of her husband, Giles," McDonnell explained. "As the stones were piled onto him, a magistrate turned to Martha, offering her a final chance to confess and spare herself."

Hanna imagined the scene: Martha watching her husband die by barbaric means—large stones being placed on the man's chest until his body broke. She wondered who could have idly watched and not said something, not wanted to save him.

McDonnell's expression darkened as he continued. "Martha begged for mercy, pleading with the judge to end her husband's torment. She cried, 'Have mercy on him— he's done nothing. I've done nothing.' But as her voice broke, the judge delivered her sentence:'Guilty.'"

Hanna leaned in, her eyes narrowing, still thinking what a horrible occupation her father had created. She wondered how the moment wouldn't have elicited more than a stoic, binary response.

"Here's where the anomaly appeared," McDonnell said. "The word 'Guilty' stuttered. It broke mid-sentence, shifted to 'Innocent,' then back again. The system glitched, flickering as if... as if even the verdict itself were conflicted."

"It couldn't commit to a decision?" Hanna asked, her tone growing tense.

McDonnell nodded. "The judge's face froze for a moment, eyes flickering—as if he, or the system, was struggling to resolve her fate. Eventually, it froze. Like it was waiting."

"If the system already knows the answer..." Hanna started to say but stopped herself. She bit at the corner of her lip, thinking, "... what could give it pause?"

McDonnell shrugged. "Thompson only said it didn't continue until he selected 'Guilty' from the options. Then it continued forward as though nothing had happened."

Hanna tilted her head, squinting at the screen, looking for some overlooked detail and finding nothing but pixels.

McDonnell swiped to the next marker: Rosa Parks (1955). Hanna raised an eyebrow. A thought hovered on her lips, a fraction of a moment lost in her own memories.

"The bus driver approached Parks but, instead of delivering the command to move, he stopped, then walked back to his seat," McDonnell read from the notes. "A moment later, he got up and returned, repeating the approach."

"He was caught in a loop?" Hanna asked. "After a choice was made?"

"Yes. Eventually, he said 'Move,' but it took several tries, almost as if the system were fighting itself to complete the action."

Hanna's mouth tightened. "It's as if... something's interrupting it, or data is missing," she murmured. Then to McDonnell, "You know, early AI systems faced this issue, too—development would plateau, inching endlessly toward a complete *original* thought but never quite reaching it. Like—"

"Like Zeno's paradox?" McDonnell asked, finishing her sentence.

Hanna nodded, never taking her eyes off the screen, her brow still furrowed. "But this decision should be simple for a machine. It hasn't always been for us, though..." She trailed off, the thought unfinished.

McDonnell paused, clearly lost, but continued. "Right. Well... that's where last week's failsafe—uh, your name—comes in." Without missing a beat, he added, "The next one's more recent. Give me a minute to pull it up."

He started to slide the timeline forward when a scream erupted from down the hall. Hanna and McDonnell both startled at the sound, the blood-curdling scream echoing from the library.

"Thompson," McDonnell said as they rushed out of the room. The timeline, still sliding forward, sped through the 1970s, 1980s, 1990s...

Their footsteps echoed through the empty spaces as they raced down the corridor and into the library, the scream intensifying. On the floor outside the simulation entrance was Thompson. He was pulling at the closed door, half-standing.

Hanna rushed to his side as she saw blood streaming down the frame, his hand caught on the other side. McDonnell pulled open an emergency panel, smashing a release button. The door hissed open, just enough to release the arm.

Thompson's hand tumbled down with a wet thud on the concrete floor, leaving a widening pool of blood. Beside it, something small skittered across the ground—a battered pocket notebook, its pages crumpled and smeared with streaks of red.

McDonnell rushed to the man, pulling on him to stand upright. Hanna stood there staring: the blood, the severed hand, the man writhing in pain.

"Help me get him to the elevator," McDonnell said, his eyes focused on Thompson's face.

Hanna didn't move, her eyes fixed on a crimson pool spreading across the floor. All the resolve she'd mustered to get here, to be in this place, drained in that instant, her mind reeling.

"Dr. Lightman!" McDonnell said, snapping her back. Hanna and McDonnell lifted him to his feet. He screamed as they pulled him toward the central room. Hanna pressed the button, the single decision: UP. The elevator doors opened.

"His hand—" McDonnell said, pulling Thompson in. "Maybe they can..."

Hanna turned and rushed back to the library, knowing time was fleeting if there was any chance to save it. Her eyes scanned the room, quickly landing on a small blanket draped across a chair—the same chair her father would have used. The thought struck her as she reached for it: he would likely sit there, wrapped in this blanket against the chill of the bunker, his eyes pointed toward his creation, the simulation chamber, thinking. Always thinking.

Gently, she scooped up the hand, wrapping it carefully in the blanket as it absorbed the pooling blood. Her heart raced as she rushed back to the elevator, only to find the doors already closed. She tapped the UP button—nothing, pressing it again and again. The elevator was gone, making its slow ascent to the surface somewhere far above.

Hanna turned back toward the empty, lifeless corridors

behind her. The faint hum of air moved through the steel grating in the walls, a subtle draft cutting through the bunker's vast, hollow silence. She wiped blood from her face with her sleeve, looking around, suddenly struck by just how alone she was in this cavernous complex.

Out of the corner of her eye, a pulsing light on her chest caught Hanna's attention. Looking down, she noticed her nametag—the one she had meant to leave behind before the tour, a quiet act of defiance against her role in this creation. Instead, it was twisted in the folds of her jacket, the edges glowing faintly. Slowly, the realization dawned: her father's system had chosen. She was the only participant left for the simulator.

The thought took her breath; an invisible wind seemed to flow up her arms and to her cheeks, raising goosebumps like icy needles. It felt like the cold hand of her father had reached out from somewhere beyond, nudging her forward, demanding her as he always did.

Hanna considered her options: Leave—her pulse quickening at the thought, the instinct to flee surging like a spark down her spine. Or stay. Her eyes landed again on the nametag: Dr. Hanna Lightman. The system—not a person, but the Nexus—had included her honorific, quietly marking her with inevitability. It seemed to know she had spent her father's final years, and the years since, dissecting the ethics of learning systems. It seemed to recognize her voice, though small, urged the world to pause. To hold back the tide of cold indifference.

Of course it had. The Nexus *always* knew.

Her entire life had been spent under that shadow, defined by the man who created the Nexus and the legacy he cultivated with meticulous precision.

More than a handful of students, journalists, and would-be acolytes had stopped her over the years to ask, to fawn, about the work of the great doctor. They wanted the mythology, the curated genius that her father had allowed them to see.

But that wasn't the man she knew. *That* man was always calculating, his cold brilliance slicing through any semblance of warmth. And yet, his shadow followed her still, pressing against her, inescapable.

Hanna sighed, to no one in particular, and turned toward the revolving door. Then something caught her eye.

Almost hidden in the shadow was Thompson's notebook. Its worn cover was warped and torn, the corners curling inward as if trying to shrink from view. Had Thompson found the answer?

She hesitated, then crouched to pick it up, her fingers brushing the damp leather. The pages were nearly unreadable—ink blurred into rust-red smears, their edges damp and warped—but one line stood out, traced over and over again with frantic pressure: *the bias mirrors the fault.*

Her breath caught. The words stabbed at something buried deep within her.

All systems have bias, she thought, but learning systems like the Nexus were meant to transcend it—to build abstractions refined to an infinite degree, allowing for nuance. So then... What bias? What fault?

The walkway ahead narrowed like a throat closing in. A wedge of dimly lit space, the boundary between her world and the Nexus. Her father had called it the future. To Hanna, it felt more like a tomb. Each step toward it felt heavier than the last, as though the machine's cold intent was pressing down on her shoulders.

She hesitated, her hands trembling as they brushed the edge of the doorframe. Every instinct screamed at her to turn away, to let this place rot in its emptiness. But something held her. The blood. The notebook. The weight of her father's expectations. Or perhaps it was something else—a pull she couldn't quite name, one that had whispered to her over the years that only she could stand here in this moment.

This isn't about finding answers, she thought. It's about the choice—go or don't go. The stark simplicity of it felt like a trap. Hanna took a breath and stepped forward.

ACT THREE

Inside the chamber, the darkness was absolute. Hanna could barely make out the room's shape—a cylindrical vault, with no corners, no clear sense of direction. In early versions, there were goggles to wear and motion chairs to sit in, but this Nexus had improved since then, and she couldn't know what to expect from the constant march of technology and time.

"The simulation starts in ten seconds," a voice said. While it came from everywhere, the sound was delicate, finely tuned. As Hanna waited, she let her hands rest on her belly, the nervous habit turning into a motion to smooth her shirt—her fingers catching on the damp, dark blood that stained it.

A fire alarm began ringing in the distance, then the hollow sound of crashing material—rocks? No, it was something more...

Hanna's ears popped, the pressure in the room changing as a stack of ceiling tiles crashed down around her, filling the air with dust. Screaming rose in the background, and she coughed, taking in the sight of a small room. The door was closed, glass windows around her cracked as if the whole building had lurched, stressing them. Hanna fought her way around a desk to the door, but it wouldn't budge. It, too, had absorbed the weight of something massive above, pressing it into the neat office carpet below.

With some effort, she grabbed an office chair and threw it against a nearby window, sending glass into the adjoining space. Outside, she saw the room was filled with smoke and people running. They passed her alone or in twos, sometimes threes. Arm-in-arm, they pulled each other along, all heading in the same direction.

Wind from shattered windows on the outer wall whipped dust and smoke around her, stinging her eyes. Tears pooled at the corners, her lips dry and caked as if a fan had blasted the room with cement dust.

In her peripheral vision, a clock appeared, hovering just at the edge of her sight. It was identical to the one outside the simulation chamber. No matter how she moved, it remained there—an ever-present sentinel, a reminder that this was only a simulation. But it wasn't counting down yet. So far, she hadn't been confronted with a binary choice, just an unmoving line of zeroes.

Yet from the vibrations in the floor, the ductwork falling from above, and the screams and cries for help, this was unlike anything she could have imagined.

She made her way to the exterior wall, around toppled desks and cubicle walls. Her hands searched for a clear path. Whole sections of walls were gone, fallen away to somewhere below. As she reached the edge and leaned out to catch a breath of fresh air, she saw no ground. At every view, there were buildings below eye level, but the street was so far underneath, she couldn't see it. To do so, she'd have to extend her body out the window several feet.

The building shook from an explosion somewhere above. Her hand, holding a beam exposed through the wall, vibrated with the reverberations. Then she saw what she hoped wouldn't be the case: out the window, a massive building—a modern monolith—rose dozens of floors above, stark and gray. Through the air came the tremendous scream of an engine. She could hear the pitch of air changing as a commercial airliner, the United Airlines logo clearly visible from the side, slammed nose-first into the other building.

Hanna recoiled from the burst of fire that followed. The

explosion sent shockwaves loosening rubble all around. Then, a crunch of stone hit the side of the building nearest to the explosion. A deep rumble shook her feet—steel and concrete flexing somewhere above her head.

Hanna's stomach dropped.

The massive towers, the chaos, the impact above—she saw it all now in terrifying clarity: she was in the first tower hit, the South Tower of the World Trade Center.

Coughing and spitting dust, she made her way along the wall, stepping over debris every few feet. Her eyes searched, knowing it was somewhere—every office had one or ten of them.

On an inner wall, she spotted it—a clock hanging askew —9:06 a.m. The building would collapse in less than an hour.

Glancing up, she thought, "The timer still hasn't started."

She saw another stream of people scrambling and followed them. Their shouts and coughs directed her when she couldn't see, the air thicker with suffocating black smoke. In a few minutes, she and the others reached a doorway to the stairwell. Just inside, a metal plate read: 87th floor. Hanna looked around as people pushed past the stairs toward, if it could be found in all the smoke, the exit somewhere far below. The building would collapse in less than an hour. From this floor she might have enough time to get to the bottom and to a minimum safe distance.

As if it were next to her ear, she heard a loud beep as the clock flashed and began counting up...

0:01...0:02...

Hanging in the air, two round buttons appeared, each

with a single word above: **Escape** or **Perish.** As if accentuating their meaning, the building shook as another section of the ceiling started to crack and bend. The message was clear: get down the stairwell or be crushed.

Hanna leaned to the doorway, one hand in the air ready to press the Escape button, and froze. She could hear voices rounding the stairs below. The path was obvious even if she were to hit the button, but there was something else. Every other simulation had been about choosing the right path for some historical event, some known moment—but here there was no one else to choose for.

This decision was for her. But what was the system trying to learn from this simulation?

She breathed hard, trying to think in all the smoke. Hanna searched the room for answers.

The ceiling had started to flex downward, more fires roaring from above. Her feet moved back, further from the doorway, away from the shouts of those down the stairs, fading. Breathing, she quieted the room, the creaking of the building becoming background noise. Faintly, she heard a voice—someone calling out. A tired, raspy scream.

Hanna made her way toward it, through the smoke, scrambling over piles of rubble. And there, standing at one of the voids where floor-to-ceiling windows once held out the elements, was a man. His suit was blackened from soot, his face covered in the milk-white powder of pulverized stone. He leaned out, waving his arms wildly. He was shouting, though the wind captured his voice, carrying it high and away, never reaching the street below.

She knew this man. Not personally, but she knew his shape, his clothing. His image appeared in her mind. Through laced fingers she remembered watching videos of him, caught on camera in a moment of desperation. The image found purchase—she remembered his body flipping end over end as he jumped, falling the length of the tower to the street below.

Hanna looked at the buttons, then at the man. He continued to flail. Screams came out like an animal entering an abattoir, knowing it wouldn't make it to the end of the corridor alive. His screams, like the animal's, weren't about escape but to get someone—anyone's—attention.

01:32…01:33…

As she approached, the ceiling behind her collapsed—pipes and cement falling in great heaps to the floor. Then, through it, revealing the floor below. She squinted, looking through the dust, coughing, to see if there might be a path back to the doorway and the stairs beyond.

01:43…01:44…

She looked again at the man, gripping tightly to the crumbling wall. She watched the tears streaming down his face with every shout into the void, wild and unrestrained.

01:46…01:47…

Then, she saw a rip in his pants, neatly torn from calf to somewhere above his knee. It didn't flap in the wind like the rest of his clothing because blood had already begun to clot, holding the pants close, wrapping a wound beneath. She saw him bobble, holding his weight with the other leg. Then she saw the bone, twisted and poking through the skin, protruding, as blood wet the fabric in another gush. So amped with adrenaline, he was standing, steadying himself on a compound fracture—a twist of broken bones finding sunlight through his skin for the first time.

Her father's binary, his unflinching calculus—none of it seemed to matter now. This wasn't about her survival, or even the choice between living or dying. She felt herself drawn forward by something outside of logic.

The timer counted up, each second a drumbeat of urgency. She stared at the buttons: *Escape* or *Perish*. To live or to die. The choice was laughably simple for a machine, so certain it could distill a human life into this binary. Her father would have admired its stark reasoning. But could this be a test for *her*?

She looked to the man beside her, helpless but fiercely alive, clinging to life.

01:59...2:00...

The sound of his screams continued to twist at her brain, stinging like the dust and smoke all around her. In his terror, she could feel her body leaning toward him, wanting to calm him, to help him.

The buttons flickered, blinking in and out. They didn't fade like she expected, but instead seemed to shudder and distort, pixels scattering and reassembling in fractured patterns. Had she done something?

02:02...02:03...

Hanna stopped moving for a moment, looking at the scene. This simulation was somehow different. Hadn't she and Thompson agreed the Nexus might be caught in a Zeno paradox—always calculating, never arriving? But what if they were wrong? What if the Nexus wasn't stuck at all?

Faced with a life-or-death choice, anyone would, of course, choose escape. Doing so would end the simulation with a clean confirmation, the expected response attained. The alternative—perishing—would be accepted just as easily, though logged by the Nexus as incorrect and locking humanity out forever.

To live or to die, Hanna thought—the words skipping through her mind, dangling like this man, teetering on the edge of a childish bias. Her father's voice echoed in her mind: *"You're here to choose."* But choose what?

At that moment, Hanna saw the fault in the system—the flaw hiding beneath its precision. This wasn't a Zeno paradox at all.

"The bias mirrors the fault," Hanna thought, the words from Thompson's notebook echoing in her mind. He had almost solved it. He had the variables in the equation but not the constants. But he didn't know what she knew. Was Thompson testing the system, triggering the glitches? Even the failsafe, she wondered?

McDonnell, too, had been right: the Nexus can calculate every probability in its memory. But that's all it could do. It couldn't feel the weight of the choice. It couldn't grasp what it meant to hesitate, to doubt, to choose for reasons that defy logic.

Her father's machine had been built to avoid the chaos of human emotion, to strip decision-making down to a cold precision. But in doing so, it had stripped away the very thing that made choices meaningful. A machine might mimic reason, but it could never grasp the humanity behind a choice.

Hanna exhaled, her chest tightening.

02:10…02:11…

Hanna's hand touched his back. She could feel the fabric of his shirt, the sweat turning cold on his skin. He spun, looking at her, his scream silenced, and she saw the tears, spread by the wind outside, carving radiating slices through the dust on his face.

She pulled at his sleeve, urging him down, putting a shoulder under his arm. His weight pulled her down as she guided him through the rubble. They both stopped as the building shook, a torrent of scalding steam hissing from the fire suppression system somewhere above.

She looked at the timer. It hadn't stopped.

02:31…02:32…

"Thank you," he whispered in her ear. Again and again, he said it like a meditation. And she thought about how it might feel to be a simulation that repeated the same moments whenever called to do so. The horror of being trapped, an unwilling but necessary participant in the theoretical game of teaching a computer that could never advance beyond a limited set of predictions.

It's watching, Hanna thought, *but could it possibly understand?*

They moved together, stepping lightly as he pulled on her. Through the smoke, now like trying to see through a chaotic snarl, she could see the doorway getting closer. In the dark stairwell, she saw a flashlight, a frenetic beam coming from a flight or two above. The beam got bigger as two men, their shirts wrapped around their faces, appeared at the doorway.

Behind her, the fire was growing, daylight locked out as the cubicles, papers, and even chairs roiled in flames.

The two men stepped in, grabbing her and the man,

pulling them toward the stairs. She let go as they took his arms, one on each side, and rushed him over the threshold and into the stairwell. The man with the fracture turned and said, one last time, "Thank you," as they disappeared into the dark.

Hanna stood, watching them go as the door slammed shut. Behind her, the room erupted in flame, heat crashing against her like a wave. The searing light blinded her, forcing her eyes shut, while the blaring sirens overwhelmed her senses, swallowing everything else. Then, silence.

When she opened her eyes again, the ever-present peripheral clock was gone. In front of her was a sliding oak door, one she instinctively recognized. This was the door to her father's study.

"...that room is dangerous," her mother had said, sometimes under her breath, sometimes aloud, and it was a sentiment Hanna shared. Dangerous. The walls held his trophies, animals frozen in fierce postures, teeth bared and claws outstretched. But that wasn't what her mother meant, was it? It was the work being done in the room—the ideas it contained—and the man who gave it all meaning. Everything he did was all or nothing without shades or nuance.

She remembered the dutiful dread of standing here, as she did now, feeling the fine hairs rise on her neck and forearms, her cheeks flushed.

<u>ACT FOUR</u>

As Hanna stepped forward, the door slid open. A manservant exited quietly with an empty tray from afternoon tea. He paid her no mind as she entered, her toes still instinctively avoiding the creaky floorboards.

From the other side of the room, she heard the booming voice of her father. "The man walks to her, his driver's cap neatly placed on his head, buttoning his coat in the winter air. He demands she stand and give up her seat. He says she'll be arrested."

Hanna stepped further in, catching sight of her younger self seated in front of her father's desk, hands absently smoothing her skirt. *Bunny,* she thought of herself then, staring at pictures of Rosa Parks, the Black woman sitting resolutely, and James Blake, the white driver. As Hanna watched, she felt a pang, a reminder of how many times she'd replayed this memory. Now, standing here, she saw herself with fresh eyes: a child, expected to shoulder the weight of his world, primed to make choices without ever understanding the full consequences.

"Can he do that?" young Hanna asked, her voice small.

"In Alabama, it's the law of the land," Dr. Lightman responded.

The young girl considered the scenario, her eyes scanning the images before she looked at a small clock on the desk, ticking up: 2:10...2:11...

"Stay...or Move?" young Hanna said, almost as a whisper. Dr. Lightman nodded, his attention moving to a sheet on his desk, studying the outcomes of previous questions. Each was recorded with a tick mark, always binary.

Young Hanna's brow furrowed as she hesitated. "What if he decided—"

Dr. Lightman interrupted,"—there is only one right choice, Hanna," her proper name cutting through his usual coaxing tone, impatience creeping into his voice. He glanced at the clock, his fingers tapping the desk in a steady rhythm. "History demands clarity. You're here to choose—not to speculate."

"But... how..." young Hanna asked, her voice barely a whisper.

Dr. Lightman punctuated his response by tapping his pen sharply on the desk, the sound filling the room. "We're not here to rewrite history, Hanna. This *will* be factual."

Young Hanna's expression fell, her posture shrinking under his scrutiny. She shifted her gaze downward, trying to suppress her doubt.

"Bunny..." Dr. Lightman's voice wrapped around the pet name with a practiced gentleness—a false softness that Hanna, listening from across time, recognized all too well. "Your quick, intuitive decisions are crucial—the ones only a child could make. You, Hanna, you'll be the central morality engine, the beating heart of the entire Nexus."

The older Hanna now stood at the edge of the desk, watching the two of them. She saw her father's face, slightly reddened as he stirred his tea, the false warmth of his pleading tone, his control masked as kindness.

"Stay," young Hanna whispered, defeated. She turned her face downward, dutiful, tears weakly clinging to her eyes.

Hanna's heart broke for this younger version of herself. She remembered the turmoil, those moments when her voice, her will to speak up, would always falter in his presence. Gently, she reached out, touching the girl's shoulder. Young Hanna looked up, seeing her, yet not fully recognizing her.

Dr. Lightman noticed her presence too, his brow rising as he studied her face with a hint of surprise—even, perhaps, a touch of softness.

"What were you going to say?" Hanna asked her younger self, her voice steady, inviting.

Tears finally fell, tumbling down young Hanna's cheeks. She looked to Dr. Lightman, then to the picture of the driver and Ms. Parks. She sniffed, holding back another wave of tears, sensing a rare moment where her voice might actually be heard.

"What if the driver didn't ask her to move? I don't know…" She took a shaky breath, her gaze shifting to her older self as if seeking reassurance. "What if…"

Hanna nodded, her voice warm. "Go ahead."

Watching this moment, Hanna felt a familiar chill run up her spine—a fear she had carried for years as her father cherished his creation more than his child. He was so consumed by what could be, he disregarded what was right in front of him. This was how she remembered him—not the saintly, oil-painted visage in the library, but this man whose control was disguised as kindness, his calculated demeanor, one she once mistook for love.

Young Hanna swallowed, her voice tentative. "What if… people just tried to be kind?"

The countdown timer buzzed, loud and unyielding. Three minutes. The bell rang as everything in the room seemed to stop moving all at once, frozen.

Two buttons appeared: **Continue** or **Shut Down.**

The older Hanna looked at them, her eyes now seeing through the binary choice.

Dr. Lightman's face changed as he watched her—his composure faltered, replaced by something new, the lines on his face seemed deeper, like worn circuitry, betraying the years devoted to his creation. His voice, usually so assured, barely a whisper: "Bunny?" It came out almost as a breath.

They watched each other for a moment as his eyes drifted to the buttons. She had never seen that expression before. Was it... fear?

Hanna exhaled, her hand trembling as it hovered in the air. She locked eyes with him, her voice steady and unyielding. "Dad, compassion can't be programmed. Maybe you understood that all along?"

With quiet resolve, Hanna pressed *Shut Down*.

A low hum faded into silence, leaving only the sound of her steady breathing in the stillness.

Hanna moved through the library, her steps measured, as the enigmatic gaze of its creator, Dr. Warren Lightman, slipped away behind her. As she stepped to the end of the corridor, the lights turned off one by one.

Hanna pressed the only button: **UP.**

READ MORE STORIES FROM THE MIDNIGHT VAULT
HTTPS://BOOKS2READ.COM/THEMIDNIGHTVAULT

ISLA

EXCLUSIVE PREVIEW

Pop fresh batteries into your Walkman and follow twelve-year-old George Perez from Chicago to the Yucatán coast, where myth isn't as dead as it seems.

With every step, the line blurs further between memory, music, and a history he can't ignore.

Week by week, the myth reveals itself at
TinyWorlds.substack.com

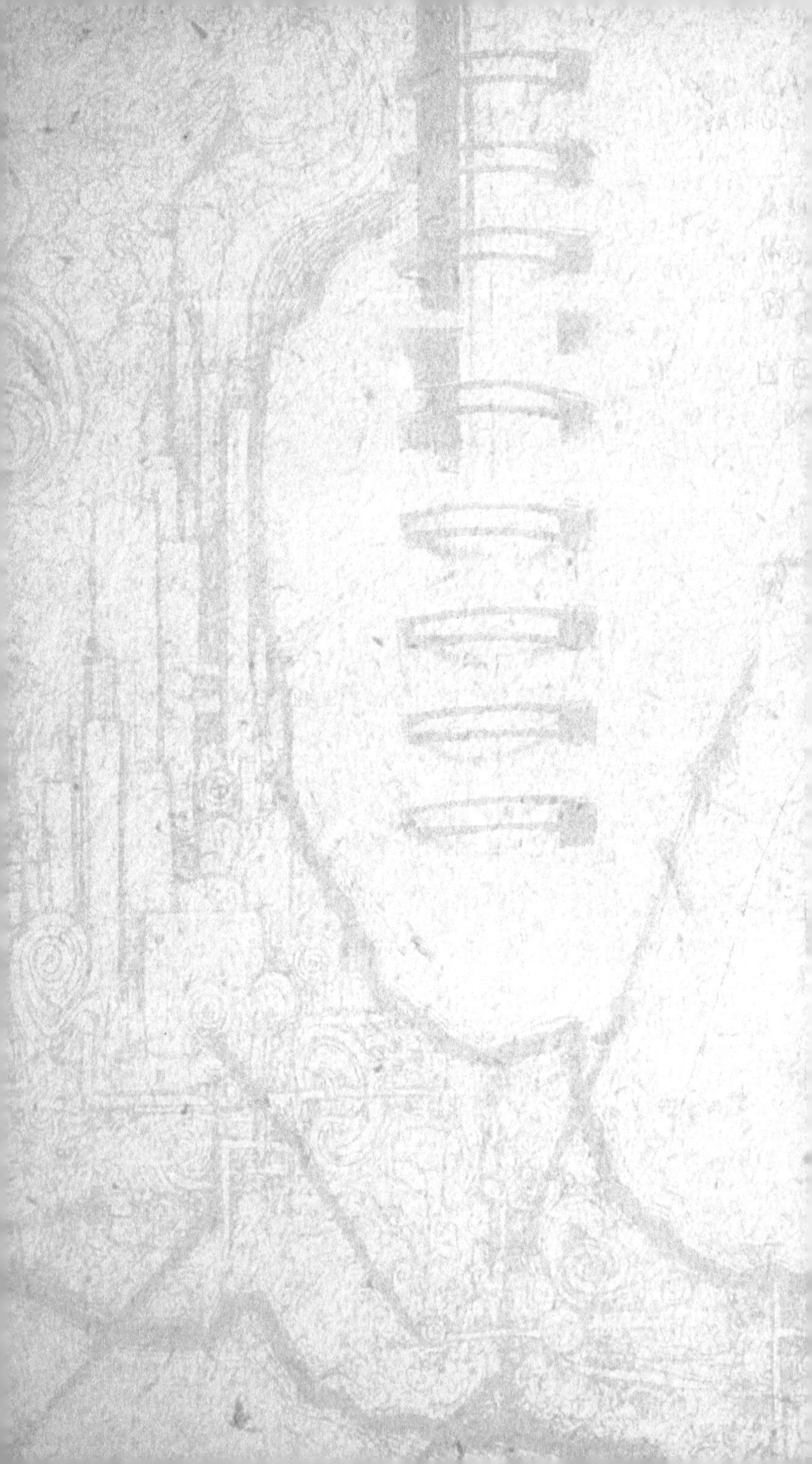

CHAPTER ONE

SNAKES, JOLT AND THE CITY

January 1986

When the hissing started, George thought of snakes—sharp and mean through the apartment walls. Even at twelve, he knew the warning always came before the strike.

Snakes hiss, right? In *Raiders* they did. His mother and the fella were in the hallway outside his room. He pictured them with fingers pointed like fangs, voices coiled and tense—like the knot in his stomach.

Fella—that's what George called them, as in "her fella" or "that fella." A generic, white box way to keep his mental Rolodex from overfilling with forgettable details, forgettable people. They were never dad, daddy, or father.

No way George was going out there. "Asps, very dangerous. You go first." Sallah told Indy. *Right on.* He wondered how long it would be before they'd strike.

George heard all the fights. The loud ones echoing in the lobby, riding with them up the elevator, then spilling into the apartment. The silent ones, simmering at the dinner table. And now, from his room, the voices writhed under the door, spilling onto his abandoned homework.

In the quiet, after an argument, his father would have raised his eyebrows, winking and said in a sing-song way:

This ain't no party,
This ain't no disco,
this ain't no foolin' around

George waited, sensing the coming crescendo, but not wishing for it. Wishing away nice things seemed rude and, well, this apartment was pretty nice. Except for the Betamax —renting a new movie sucked, there was never one he wanted and he'd take home The Last Starfighter for the hundredth time. He thought about it for a minute: he'd take an escape into space right now. He didn't even have to be chosen to do something daring or extraordinary.

It all belonged to the fella, of course. The apartment was big enough to have a real dining room and a decent view of the city. His mom called it "yuppy modern," with its sparse decor and chairs made out of thick plastic that looked like glass. The fella's espresso machine was a work of art, too. He shined it every morning as it spat black sludge into tiny cups.

George detested the stuff—he was a Jolt cola drinker. "All the sugar and twice the caffeine," the ads said. Heck yeah. Maybe it really was just carbonated coffee, but it got him from here to there—quickly—he thought. He even liked the jitter it gave him as the chemicals pushed through his veins. It got him through the Chicago snow, past the suits, onto the city bus and, at least, halfway through the day.

He liked that it made him feel wide-eyed, a rush. He'd

blink, and it'd be third period already—Mrs. Romey talking while his pencil drifted into its own language. George wasn't listening while she went on about Mesoamerican civilizations. Not really. His pencil carved spirals and half-formed shapes in the corner of his worksheet, each one hovering off the page, alive. The names blurred—Olmec, Zapotec, Maya—and in his head, Siouxsie cut through them like a blade, chanting something strange and holy:

We're spellbound... spellbound... spellbound...

The teacher asks a question, it's clear nobody is going to answer.

"George?"

"Toltec," he muttered. Then he kept drawing, his hand shaping a mountain, maybe a cave.

He wasn't even sure why he said it. It just... came out. Not exactly a memory, more like muscle memory. Maybe it didn't matter. Most of the other kids never get called on anyway–they were continuously tuned out, or jacked up. Some were into more harsh things than caffeine. Before the first bell he'd see them in the bathroom sniffing or puffing something–not George's style. He preferred the minor infraction of a Jolt cola at dawn. Music playing in his head-phones he'd whisper *Dead Kennedys* lyrics as the hot wizz of Jolt hit the urinal.

With a fountain of fads
more rock and roll ads
drug me, drug me, drug me-me-me

The bell must've rung. Now it was Kathryn and the fella, not teachers and kids—voices louder, closer, tumbling over his bed. How many other kids had lived in three different cities by age twelve? He had a good idea what would happen next—it was probably time for a trip to the Grand Canyon State, to the retirement villa with a movie theater and all-you-can-eat buffet. He could already picture himself, his bike pedaling faster than the golf carts now. Kathryn would want the retreat, but did he have to go?

Could he go out there right now and stop her from saying the words?

Better yet—could he stay right here and use his tele-pathic powers to cool her down? *Or was that telekinetic?* Which one made people's heads explode? George closed his eyes and leaned his head toward the door. From the safety of his room maybe he could invent one of those powers, the right one, now?

Maybe she'd freeze mid-sentence. Circuits snapping behind her eyes. Her head slumps. Body goes slack. The fella leans in, confused. He starts to apologize. He raises his hand to pound the wall. Maybe even cry a little.

Then: *whirrrr*. Her eyes flick open. Glowing red.

She grabs the fella's throat, lifts him like The Terminator, slams him against the hallway wall, feet dangling, breath wheezing out.

George sighed.

Yeah. No stopping it. A trip to the desert was as inevitable as hot seatbelts and old lady perfume.

He looked around the room, the walls feeling closer than usual, like someone squeezing a tube of toothpaste from both ends.

As bedrooms went, it wasn't shabby—bed, lamp, closet, the usual—but for George, bedrooms had to be more than that. They were where you retreated when the world didn't make sense. They were escape pods. Pressure valves. Places that didn't ask questions.

This one had a window. Not that it mattered much. The city view from this side was only a crowd of buildings leaning into each other like they were waiting in a lunch line.

But the light came in differently.

The room had felt dull until he started taping up his drawings—ripped from his sketchpad, fuzzy at the edges. He placed them without any plan, a loose constellation across the wall. A man standing outside a café, cross-hatched shadows stretched under his feet. A cactus catching morning light, spines drawn like radiating threads. A crab mid-scuttle. A wave curling.

When he stood back, the afternoon sun tilted through the glass—off, somehow, the wrong angle for the time of day. But it moved across the drawings anyway. Not just lit them–touched them.

The smoke from the café drawing bent in a breeze that didn't exist. Sand on the beach sketch seemed to shift. The glint off the cactus looked wet.

And in the center of it all, the self-portrait.

Unfinished. Smudged from too many tries. Paper buckled where he'd erased the eyes again and again. But this version—half-done, almost accidental—was the one that looked the most like him. It followed the shape of his face. Studied him back. Its charcoal eye, dark and sharp, flickered. Just once.

He hadn't thought much about them while he made them but now, lined up like this, they felt like coordinates. Not directions to follow but... something.

He blinked. The fight was back.

Outside his room, it was now up a notch—intense, a

scrambled pay channel kids weren't supposed to see. A death match. George's mother, Kathryn, knew how to circle, how to set up the fatal blow.

There was a time, not that long ago, when her laugh came easier—when she'd dance in the kitchen or sing off-key in the car just to make him laugh. That Kathryn was still in there somewhere, but she'd gotten quieter with every move, every goodbye.

He thought he could see shadows playing along the threshold of the door—two wrestlers in an epic battle. One clinging to the ropes for life. The other undefeated. She keenly hid her weapon, like a blade in a boot. Kathryn, the relationship assassin, always knew when to pull out the knife—and more importantly, where to put it.

Then he heard it. Kathryn's preamble had started.

Kathryn—never Kate, Katie, or Kay—kept track of every transgression, every fumbled moment. She could recite, as she was doing now, the exact date and time she should have pulled the brake. Word by word, her voice gained speed, steady as the clack-clack of a runaway train. The fella might try to jump in, but she'd carry on. George had heard it enough to know the cadence, the shape of the thing. He could mouth the words as they arrived—hers at full volume, his at a whisper: "This isn't working for anyone."

He reached under the bed, tugging at the edge of a shoe-box. Inside: rows of cassette tapes, arranged with care. Some still pristine in their jewel cases—New Order, Bad Brains, XTC, The Clash. And, of course, all four Peter Gabriel albums: Car, Scratch, Melt, Security. The rest were a rattle of loose cassettes, mixtapes featuring Siouxsie Sioux, Dead Kennedys, The Smiths—half-labeled, but unmistakable.

He grabbed one. Not an original, just a dub. Next to the Memorex logo, in blocky, robotic handwriting: REPLICAS.

He slid it into the Walkman and closed the door with a satisfying schnick—the sound of an armature locking into place, the magnetic head pressing against exposed tape. That sound meant escape. His Walkman. His headphones with their soft foam covers. This was the feeling of—he searched for the word—control. There wasn't enough of that to go around, but this... this was his.

His thumb pressed Play. A track was fading out—an undulating synth line, like a sci-fi film unspooling behind his eyelids. The next came in heavier: a computerized tuba in a marching band, sharp and synthetic. George closed his eyes, turning up the volume, drowning out the argument.

It's cold outside
And the paint's peeling off of my walls
There's a man outside
In a long coat, grey hat
smoking a cigarette
Now the light fades out
And I wonder what I'm doing in a room like this

He could see the shapes outside his door had gone still.

He finished putting the room into his mental Rolodex: textbooks on the floor. His artwork on the wall. The way streetlights sneaked in through the snow.

He slid the box of cassettes into his backpack, then his sketchbook and a box of pencils. Then he paused. There was still room. And something missing.

He pulled open the drawer of his nightstand. He hadn't looked for it in months, but he knew exactly where it was: his father's journal.

He brushed the dust off the cover. The leather was softer now, darker, worn smooth from being dragged across too many state lines. It still smelled like ink and old paper. Like something that didn't quite belong anywhere, but always ended up with him.

You don't always know why you keep something—it just stays close. Or maybe you follow it.

A folded paper slipped out of the journal and landed on the floor. A map.

He didn't open it, but he saw his own handwriting near the edge, pointing toward an island. Just far enough inside the fold to vanish from view—but he knew it was there. He remembered the curve he'd spotted on the old xerox. The one that looked like a smudge, a printer's mistake. *Pez doblado.*

He could almost hear his dad's voice, distant but clear: "Maps don't show the world as it is, Jorge. They show how someone imagined it might be."

George ran a finger over the journal's spine, then slipped it into his backpack.

Tomorrow is moving day.

CHAPTER TWO
THE TICKING BEGINS

THE WHEELS ON THE BUS GO... *KA-FLUMP*, BOUNCING OVER THE break between concrete road and bridge. That sound leads into a long buzz with a series of incremental *tick-tick*s as the wheels roll over the metal grating.

Bridges make the most interesting sounds, George thinks. It reminds him of a Love and Rockets song he can't quite remember—something with a clock-like ticking. That sound seems to follow him, a continuation of the feeling he'd had all night as he watched the buildings outside for any change in the light.

He'd barely fallen asleep when he felt the soft rub on his shoulder. Kathryn had her bag at the door. The fella was nowhere in sight. So much the better, George thought.

"I try to..." is all George catches from Kathryn as he slips on his headphones.

It feels like a crappy thing to do, but sometimes the world has to be tuned out.

Sometimes he doesn't even play music, like now—a barrier of subtle autonomy. She continues for a moment until she sees he's not listening. He'll have to listen at some point, but not now. She'll want to talk about what wasn't working, why the fella wasn't the right one. She'll apologize, and mean it.

But here they are: not in a car or a cab, but on a bus, bags at their feet and bundled up like alpine hikers. The rest of their belongings—just a few boxes of mostly forgotten things—will arrive later. Probably stored in the garage next to his grandparents' Pontiac Grand Prix until... wherever next.

George scans the buildings through the big windows of the bus and wonders why the lights are on at Wrigley Field. He imagines the sharp, echoing crack of a bat—it's only the sound of another promise splitting in half. One more added to the Rolodex.

Mom. Mother. Kathryn. As exacting as she could be about her name, that same magnifying glass got hazy with men. The fellas. They come and go, leaving mostly a memory of knee-down talks with "the little man." George cataloged a few of them. They all start with a friendly, "buddy" or "pal" or "kiddo."

"It's not your fault" was by far the most frequent. George considers the serious money he'd have by betting on that one. Followed closely was, "too bad we won't get to ______."

George's mind, like Kathryn's, remembers them all as he flicks through the Mad Libs answers: *see the zoo, go fishing, build a treehouse.* Maybe *see a game at Wrigley Field* should be added to the list.

Even at his age, he knows these speeches were a sympathy ploy. After all, who wants to be rejected? Why not let fly with all the loose change you can throw at a moment?

But it was also just chest-thumping, wasn't it? An adult male version of "See what I can do!" George thought of the chimps on *Wild Kingdom*—their wide mouths letting out toothy mating calls. They beat their chests for attention.

Chimps? Chumps.

George pushes out a sigh. Hot breath fogs the bus window. The world outside turns hazy as streetlights, headlights, and lit signs diffuse in the condensation. His finger reaches up to draw a shape in the mist: a long rectangle. Then a couple of triangles. Another triangle, a tail.

The airplane takes shape—its wings cast back. He adds wind in swirls racing over the cockpit. And all the while he's thinking about that relentless clock. And Arizona. Did he really have to go? Could this trip be skipped or...

Plane assembled, he begins to outline a new shape. He breathes on the window again, expanding his canvas. The condensation from his fingertips leaves beads of water streaking in jagged patterns as the bus bumps up and down.

His knee bumps the pack. He knows it's in there—the journal, folded map and all—pressed against a box of pencils. For a second, it feels like the whole bag is vibrating, howling at him. Like something inside it wants to get out. And, for a moment, he thinks maybe he shouldn't have looked at the journal, fed it, after midnight. George chuckles to himself, the hot huff of air adding to his misty canvas.

He adds a fire in quick flicks, flames engulfing the tail. A marshmallow left too long on the campfire. George draws windows—far too big for an actual plane. In one, he writes HELP.

A rough map of the United States appears in his swirls—the airplane high above as he adds speed lines to it.

This plane is not going fast. It's going down. In a hurry.

But where? Into the swamps of Louisiana? Will it skitter across the waves in the Gulf of...

George hears the plane careening, engines in a dive.

With moments left to find a safe place, the pilot comes over the intercom. His calm voice crackles with just a hint of a smile: "Ladies and gentlemen, this is your pilot… it's now or never if you want to jump out."

He breathes at the drawing, nose to the glass, looking out to the morning and the airport just beyond. The low groan of the bus brakes cuts through the air as passengers lean in a soft sway, adjusting to the stop. George stares at the plane for a moment longer, wondering: was it going down or just waiting to be saved?

He's not sure. Standing, he wipes the image away with his sleeve.

CHAPTER THREE
VOICE OF LEGENDS

September 1983

Outside the radio station, a warped sign hung over the entrance, its faded letters—KIXL—barely clinging to the metal. Beneath it, the old speaker crackled to life, sharp and sudden. George jumped, every time. He told himself it shouldn't scare him—students had blown it long ago turning the sidewalk into a dance floor, but still, it got him.

Tonight, as he listened to the incoherent noise spilling from it, he caught a pattern. *Yeah, he knew it.* He also knew exactly who was behind the microphone. And that rhythmic buzzing—the kind that made the speaker rattle just so— could only be *Bonzo.*

Kathryn opened the door, holding George back as a waft of smoke came tumbling out. Inside, the waiting area George's father called *Charon's Stop* was plastered with musical detritus: concert posters and music zines taped, tacked, and glued to the walls; a dozen records, cracked and nailed to the wall with a duct tape sign that read "Disco Sucks." Anyone who had spent time at the college station had offered some kind of knick-knack to the altar of the waiting room. Buried somewhere on the wall was Hendrix with his Hindu-inspired multiple heads, eyes peeking out from between a leaflet that promised "Weight Loss Now, Ask Me How!" and a grease-penciled endowed pinup of Burt Reynolds. He wasn't sure why but it made him blush.

The welcoming but ratty couch was always occupied, night or day, by whoever was next to take over the station.

Immediately, his eyes caught sight of six stark-white sneakers on the floor. A Black guy—dark as midnight—grinned at the sight of a kid stepping into such a disheveled place. Maybe he looked darker because of the two pale white guys on either side.

George regarded them for a moment, noticing that all three were wearing identical striped tracksuits. To him, they looked kind of silly—like maybe they were heading to a sleepover or something.

As George and Kathryn wound through the narrow halls of the studio, the music from the main control room grew louder. The ear-splitting sound of John Bonham's drums banged off the walls, along with the galloping thunder of John Paul Jones, the frenetic wails of Jimmy Page, and, of course, the screaming voice of Robert Plant who sings...

Oh, the mighty arms of Atlas
Hold the heavens from the Earth

Behind a sound console, the technician's head throbs back and forth in time with the music, trance-like, hair hanging long over his bearded face. A few others are crowded into the small room, oblivious to the entrance of George and Kathryn.

The last triplets of the song ring out and the technician

comes to, pointing to the glass on the other side of the console as the music fades. Inside we hear a voice, equally booming as Bonham's drums: George's father.

In his element behind a microphone, he leans in and says, "Did you hear that? '*Oh, the fun to have, to live the dreams we always had.*' The mighty Zep isn't just playing—they're poking you in the chest, telling you to get out there. The punished Atlas is holding up the heavens, keeping them from crashing down on your head. They're saying the road ahead is yours—treacherous and full of pitfalls, but yours!"

He flips his pages of notes in the air, letting them flutter this way and that, laughing, and shouted, "Holy moley!"

It was as if the heavens have just passed down the great word from on high, to Led Zeppelin and through him.

George smiles at this, his father so animated. He likes this version. It's an act, of course, but not a far step from the man who wakes up, groggy-eyed looking for his coffee mug, doing his Igor impression from *Young Frankenstein*, "Walk this way." George would step in behind him pretending to hold a cane.

Leaning to the mic, his father continues with a steady intensity, "That bell is ringing for you. Why? *We* are the queens and the kings—not because we wear crowns, but because something ancient still moves in us. Mythology isn't dead—it's a rhyme that still echoes today. The old stories keep speaking, because the spirits in them haven't departed."

He pauses, ensuring his words sink in, "As we're pouring over the myths, our history, searching out for the truth of what lies beyond, we're also shaping it."

His voice lowers, his tone conspiratorial, "Remember, we're not meant to hunt for immortal treasures from behind a desk, but to touch the land and ask it what it remembers. We should be out there—yes, to steal fire, but also to listen for its crackle and to stoke that flame for others. To go down into the mines and face the Balrog—not for glory, but as keepers of a legacy that's never really left us, to carry on what was started."

From the back of a classroom or here in the sound booth, George sees a familiar spark in his father's eyes as he spins in the DJ chair. It reminds George of his Blue Oyster Cult t-shirt, the one with the stretched-out neck and sleeves, broken in just right. His father wears this presence as naturally as that shirt, like it's part of him.

George wonders if he has that in him, to be this vivid, to have a classroom—or a whole town full of people—leaning in, listening, like his father does. Could he step forward and command that kind of attention, or would he fade into the background? His father makes it look effortless, but would anyone listen to George the same way?

George waves into the window as Kathryn steps closer, smiling—a small, knowing smile, like she's seen this performance a hundred times. His father catches sight of them and smiles through the glass of the recording booth. He lets the silence hang, drawing in his audience, then gives George a slow, deliberate wink before continuing.

"It's your turn to wield the hammers and the axes, to write the next sagas, and take the world in your hands. But don't forget—some of the gods are still out there. Still watching. Still fighting for us. Like the Hero Twins, who never stopped tricking the lords of the underworld. Their story didn't end. And even with their help, it's we mortals who must rise—our actions bold enough to echo forward through time. You better believe it."

The sound engineer pops a tape cart into the machine

and begins the opening organ and drums of Pink Floyd's *Eclipse*:

all that you touch, all that you see...

"So, who among you will bring new adventures—those vast tales that will be written in books or retold as bawdy barroom legends, passed from voice to voice, long after we're gone? I hope you're listening, because the world needs your adventure. Needs your spirit."

And all you create, and all you destroy...

"That's all for tonight. We've traversed the plane of the gods, stolen fire from Olympus, and come back down to Earth changed. I'm your host, Professor Perez. To my new students... Yes, tomorrow we take on the heroes—*Achilles, Beowulf, Odysseus*. Legends? Maybe. Flawed? Absolutely. I hope you've done your reading." He laughs, "Until we meet again, keep the legends alive and let the music guide you. Goodnight and safe travels through the ages."

Everything under the sun is in tune
But the sun is eclipsed by the moon

———

George let his mop of hair blow in the wind as he sits in the back of the Triumph. With the top down and his body twisted into the lunchbox-sized space behind the seats, there wasn't much he could do about it anyway. He didn't mind. If George wanted to, he could probably reach the steering wheel or even lean over to touch the ground—the car was that small. It wasn't uncommon for his father to bark, "Down, Jorge!" so he could see through the rearview mirror.

Usually, after the show, his father was talkative, animated, full of lingering electricity from the station. But tonight, the air felt flat. Even on a fall night, when that charge might otherwise buoy them against the chill, something was different.

George noticed it first in his father's shoulders—tense, arms locked stiff to the wheel. Then in the way he ground the gears, how the car's suspension bottomed out when they left the parking lot.

"Should we be worried? I mean, if it comes down to it, I can find something more stable." Kathryn says, pulling her hair back as the wind whips through it.

His father shrugged, unsure—a small motion, but one that felt like he was trying to shift the weight off his shoulders, even for a second. Taking a quick glance in the mirror his eyes meet George's.

"I mean, you can pick up other classes, maybe amend your syllabus..." Kathryn suggests, letting the thought hang for him to catch.

"Sure, but that's not the point, is it? The provost has his head so far up Naisbitt's ass he's taking those pop-futurist predictions as gospel. *Megatrends*? The Enola Gay couldn't carry the megatons of crap that guy is selling."

George watches the conversation volley back and forth, unsure what any of this means. In the booth, his father's voice had filled the room, big and sure, like he knew everything. But here, in the car, he was quiet. Smaller.

"What worries me," his father pauses, reflecting, "is that we're trading an entire human history of literature for quick cash to bolster something as superficial as computer programming. They want me to funnel more kids into lesser classes." He shakes his head, downshifting hard. The gears grind, and George catches the slight wince at the corners of his father's eyes. "We're sacrificing depth for breadth. These kids don't even realize they're about to walk into the house of razors—not that they'll understand that reference much longer."

"Are you going to give me the *'mythology is our cultural mortar'* speech?" Kathryn asks, a frown forming before she forces a small smile. "I think I already took that class."

His father turns to her, holding her gaze just a moment too long. The Spitfire seems to steer itself as the road narrows around them. Kathryn knows she's stepped close to a landmine. George sees his father's jaw tighten, his tongue touching his top lip as he prepares his reaction.

"You think the future is just everyone chained to computers, like it's inevitable?" He laughs, shaking his head. "And then what? The slope gets pretty damn slippery, Kathryn. Are we going to have kids living out their whole lives inside computer simulations? Never learning to separate fact from fiction, heroes from villains?"

"It's not computers..." Kathryn says. "It's progress that scares you."

His father shrugs, as if the words don't reach him. He checks the mirrors for nothing important. His fingers brush the radio dial, tapping it, then pulling back.

"Maybe we should take a break," he says. "Head to Mexico or Guatemala. Lay low. I'll finish my research. Show George the ruins."

George hears this, his head tilting just enough between the seats to eavesdrop, avoiding the road noise, the wind.

"What? And live in the dirt for a few months? A few years?" Kathryn asks, her eyes locked on him now. George watches the way his father grips the wheel, eyes somewhere ahead, a fifty-yard stare.

As the road unwinds in front of them, Kathryn thinks of the other conversations they've had in this car—caught in the rain when the top wouldn't go up, or in full sun as they crossed into the city for lunch. Of when George was small enough to lay flat in the back, happy to be anywhere—at the beach or in the mountains, swimming in the chilly summer waters of Castle Lake with Mt. Shasta just over the ridge.

And even before George, just the two of them—young and unmoored, chasing ghost towns and roadside diners, sleeping under the stars in a borrowed tent, inventing a life with no map.

She sees him now—her partner in every sense—wrestling with the compounding interest of family life, of work he enjoys but that's starting to yield diminishing returns. She recognizes the faraway look in his eyes, not just a reflection of the road ahead, but of a man contemplating deeper crossroads. She sees him staring at the once-bright lights of youth and purpose, watching them flicker under the weight of reality.

But she doesn't say any of this. Not out of fear, but because she knows he needs time to peel away the dried onion layers. She knows, believes, that the softer skin is beneath, and he'll find it when he's ready.

Kathryn reaches over and places her hand on the back of his.

George leans in, this time crossing the narrow space between the headrests, drawn into the quiet. He looks to his parents, both staring ahead, the engine sputtering beneath them.

"Are we moving?" he asks.

His father comes to, his eyes refocusing on the moment, on his son.

"No, mijo," he says. "Times are hard out there for dreamers, Jorge."

George studies his father in the mirror, waiting for the glance. When it comes, his father adds,

"But I've got something good for bedtime. One from the vault."

The Triumph slips through the city, quiet now, the engine humming low and steady all the way home.

Street lamps flicker past in blurred patterns. The wind lifts over the windshield and tumbles through George's hair, carrying with it the coming scent of winter and something older.

CHAPTER FOUR

THE BEDTIME STORY

"The cave stinks like stale, wet laundry. We'd spent weeks hiking all over the Yucatán and were used to the damp, rotting smell of the jungle, but this was something else entirely. Locals said the island was cursed—bad things happened when you stayed too long. The air definitely felt heavier here, like it knew something we didn't. And it was no cooler inside. The walls were covered in a layer of moss that became thick with slimy hair the farther we walked."

George's father had told countless stories–mythic, dramatic, larger than life–but never this one. Just imagining the smell made George's nose wrinkle.

"Down we went, deeper and darker, until even the last sliver of daylight vanished behind us. It felt like the cave had swallowed every trace of light. We couldn't see a thing, but our ears told us we were in a massive room. My guide and translator, a man I called Hermano, paused, listening—he could hear water trickling down the walls. Then he rummaged through his pack for a flashlight."

His voice dropped, almost like sharing a secret, "Hermano was always more prepared than me."

"When it sputtered to life, we saw we were standing on a ledge. Beyond us, nothing—just a vast, open black. It didn't feel empty. It felt ancient, like something older than the jungle was waiting inside it. I knelt and scooped up a few stones."

Holding a leather book in one hand, his father reached down with the other, fingers brushing the shag carpet of the boy's room. "And threw them."

The pebbles sailed through the air. George saw them arc past his dresser, over the clothes slouched on the edge of the laundry basket, and disappear into the deep.

"A few hit the walls, some skittered forward. Tink-tink. Then, after a long pause, we heard them bounce far below —so deep the light couldn't touch it. We could only see a few feet ahead.

Catching a glimpse of the leather journal as the page turned, George tried to read ahead. The handwriting was neat and angular, but barely legible to him.

"'El tesoro?' Hermano asked in a whisper, pointing down."

"Treasure?" the boy asked.

"Maybe." Setting the journal aside, his father looked at him, their eyes meeting in the dimly lit room. "Everyone's always chasing gold, looking for something glittering in the dark. But what if they're wrong. What if the real treasure was something else entirely?"

The boy's eyes widened, as if to say, "What could be more valuable than gold?"

"What if–"

"Did you have a map?" George interrupted.

His father laughed. "This isn't 'X marks the spot'—there is no spot. Just riddles and rumors. There's history carved into temples and stelae, but most of it we still can't read.

And remember, the Spanish burned almost everything the Maya ever wrote—thousands of books, gone. What survived became an oral history, passed down like memory songs. Like in *Fahrenheit 451*—when the pages are gone, the people become the books. We followed what scraps we could. Honestly, just finding the island was a miracle."

There are no pictures of this adventure—not even a Polaroid. Just the images his father's voice painted, flickering like a film reel in George's mind. He sees him—tanned and young, like Indiana Jones. No, not quite. More like Indiana Pérez, the Mexican version.

George sinks deeper, not just hearing the story but stepping into it. He sees his father and Hermano paddling across the water, the island growing larger as the mainland slips away. Then the jungle—slashing at vines with machetes, the sky dimming to twilight, stars pricking through the canopy overhead. His eyes go wide, imagining that kind of outside. That much sky might be too much.

He blinks, adjusting the picture behind his eyes. The sounds come next—buzzing, skittering, mosquitoes the size of his hand or his face. *No thank you. No bugs.*

Music might hide those sounds. Something big and spooky, like in the movies. A creeping symphony? No— drums. Heavy, deep, like thunder rumbling far off.

Like *Conan the Barbarian.*

Yeah. That's better.

He hears them now, echoing in his head. And down in the hot cave, he pulls the blanket tighter over his legs.

"Our path was no wider than a foot across. One wrong move, and we would've fallen to our death. We cautiously stepped forward, holding onto one another. That's when we started to hear a sound."

Snapping back from his daydream—*what sound?*

"It was like a deep, throaty roar. The farther down, the louder it became. Las voces. An incantation, a chant, something that was definitely not wind. It started echoing through the cave."

A low, deep moan comes from his father, the sound of the cave coming to life in the dark. His eyes dart to George then around like he's really there, listening, searching for the sound. George presses against his arm, forcing a smile—he doesn't want his father to think he's scared. Even though, if he's being honest, he'd rather hear a different story before bed. Something with fewer spooky caves. Fewer voices echoing in the dark.

"We finally found the bottom. The sound, whatever it was, was clearly coming from in front of us. It was then that Hermano's flashlight fizzled out, plunging us into darkness again, just at the edge of a giant pool of water."

George's shoulders tensed as his head slowly lowered down in a protective shrug.

"Once our eyes adjusted to the dark, we could see water... and a glowing river, flowing beneath the walkway. The edges of it shimmered with tiny flashes of light beneath the surface. It wasn't much, just enough light for us to see as we slowly shuffled forward toward..."

Sucking in air, George held his breath, waiting for the next words. His father paused, glanced at the book and the story ahead, then looked down at the boy and said, "Maybe that's enough for tonight..."

"Dad!?"

"You want me to keep going? Even if it gets scary?"

His mouth dry from the heat of the cave, George swallows, his tiny Adam's apple plunging. In his dim bedroom, he can see the sparkling water reflecting on the walls. The voices still echo in his head—even as music drifts in from the next room. Kathryn's music:

Stranded starfish have no place to hide
Still waiting for the swollen eastern tide

George nods—*keep going.*

His father studies him for a moment, eyes searching, like he's weighing something unspoken. George wonders what he's looking for—one of those big, silent questions he never quite knows how to answer. But beneath it, there's something steadier. Quieter. A flicker. A spark.

George feels it too. Like something is being passed to him, not just the story, but a weight, a wonder. A bundle placed in his hands. A map, maybe—its markings still invisible, waiting to be revealed.

His father opens the journal again, the leather cover curled and heavy. He thumbs through, his finger dragging down a page to find his place.

"We followed the sounds. In the darkness, I wasn't sure if my eyes were tricking me until Hermano noticed it too—a faint light ahead, like a door opened just a crack."

George's father squinted, lifting a hand to shield his face as if fending off some invisible wave. "As we got closer it hit us," he continued, his voice lower now. "A blast of hot air, like stepping too close to an open furnace. Hermano whispered that we shouldn't go any further. I could feel him leaning backward, hesitant. We could see the opening more clearly, the light and heat coming from just around a corner where the voices were coming from."

George sits up, pushing away the Empire Strikes Back comforter, the frozen safety of Hoth is no match for the story's rising heat.

"A low, throaty chant came from a room made of the mountain itself. As we craned our necks to peek inside, we saw a group standing in a circle, each holding a small glowing torch. Their faces were covered, but we could clearly see they wore long, decorative cloaks and hoods that hid their features. They surrounded a plinth made of stone. It looked to be made of the earth, with designs that circled it."

"Like a…" George interrupts, thinking about the word, "stelae?" It feels clumsy in his mouth.

"Good memory!" His father considers this, "It was definitely a marker of sorts but not carved, it was painted with intricate designs all around. Ancient and otherworldly."

"Could you read any of it?"

"A little, but I'm no expert."

George's face fell.

"Jorge, it was so hot, and we were scared out of our wits," his father said, shaking his head. "But I did see two shapes..."

Turning the leather-bound book, George leaned to get a better look. On the page were two hand-drawn pictures, traced over several times, like someone emphasizing their importance or trying to remember the details before losing them forever.

"What I could see"—he hesitated, brow furrowing—"was only a little between the figures standing there, through the empty spaces in the group."

George looked at them, studying them. "A turtle and a girl?"

"Yes. But I don't know what they mean. And my drawing isn't as good as yours, Jorge."

The boy sighed, perplexed, eyes narrowing as he turned the puzzle over in his mind. He traced the lines with his fingers. The shapes were unmistakable but only fragments. They felt like an album cover where the magic of their meaning was to be understood only when the music on the record revealed the full story.

"I've looked at other pictograms from Chichén Itzá to Guatemala and can't find a similar one," his father said, adding, "Maybe you can figure them out, Jorge."

George looked back at his father, a slight grimace on his face. He was entertained but not certain at all, at eight years old, that he was capable of such a feat. He looked back at the drawings and, trying to read his father's handwriting for more meaning, saw a single word in the text below...

"Murciélago?" George said.

His father turned the book, deciphering his own writing. "Yeah!" he said. "I'll get to that."

George pulled the covers back over his legs, still sitting up, waiting for whatever might come next.

"This was no room of treasure—at least, not the kind we expected. We had stumbled onto something ancient. A ritual maybe. And we did not feel welcome to stay and watch. Hermano pointed to a passage on the far side of the chamber. The voices rose, rhythmic and steady, but at least they masked our footsteps. We moved carefully, silent, hoping not to be noticed."

George saw a close-up of boots on the cavern floor, a few pebbles of rock quietly grinding against the floor as they stepped.

"We sneaked around the group, their voices almost an animal-like growl. They swirled up and reverberated off the walls of the cavern getting louder and louder. Sweat blurred my vision, stinging my eyes. I lost my place behind Hermano, stumbling into the wall just as we were about to slip past them. A torch on the wall crashed to the ground. Immediately they turned toward us! Inside one of the hoods, a jaguar's face stared back—burning eyes locking onto mine, through me. I froze."

Hands on his cheeks, George sees them staring at him, too.

"Hermano yanked me to my feet as I grabbed the fallen torch, holding it like a weapon. More figures turned—first a crow, then a coyote, then a quetzal. Each more terrible than the last. Then, the Jaguar growled at us, no: howled! It reached out for us, not with the arms of a man but with grotesque claws. Hermano and I ran!"

Holding the book to his chest, George's father moved side-to-side, running in place, his chest heaving.

"As we exited the chamber, the cave opened up around us. The stone path split into a bunch of directions—we didn't know which way to go. I bumped into Hermano, the torch slipping from my hands as it dropped into the water. As it sank, those sparkles in the water started swirling around it until it just vanished somewhere deep. Right then, something brushed against my cheek, and I could hear the flutter of wings..."

"The bats?!" George said.

"Yes! There was a shimmer in the air, a tiny blur of light. But not just any bat — this one was glowing! All over its back was this star-like twinkle we could see as it twisted and turned around us. It would circle us then move away making these crazy loops before coming back. Then, a swarm of them flew from the darkness, streaks of light coming from every direction and heading off into the cave."

George looked around his room, in the darkness of the cave he's watching the bats weave through the air.

"We kept expecting the, the, whatever-they-were to find us. To attack us. Hermano pointed in the direction the bats flew like they were telling us which way to go. In the dark, we followed their lights, down a long path."

George's pulse is racing with every word.

"Like guardian angels they dove down, perching in the mouth of a cave, just inches above the water. The glow on their backs was pointing the way—down, into the water! We dove in, the water all around us lit up with those tiny little lights. The cave was like an escape tunnel but the further we ventured in the passage got smaller. With seconds to decide, the only way forward was underwater. We held our breaths as the current swept us down..."

George gulps a chestful of air, holding it. Monsters. Bats. A dark cave.

"The current pushed us down and through the long caves, water sparkling all around. Hermano got pulled down a side tunnel and I lost sight of him. The cave was so rocky that I banged my head, the world was spinning and I almost lost consciousness."

Still holding his breath, the boy's eyes are wide, unblinking, incredulous.

"Finally, after what felt like minutes, the cave spit me out, somewhere far down the mountain. The beach was only a few feet away at the edge of the tidepool. I just laid there, gasping for breath."

George lets out his breath. With it comes a long, high-pitched sigh.

"When I flopped onto my back the sky was a blurry mess of blood from the gash on my head. I laid there for a few minutes catching my breath. I looked around for Hermano but he was nowhere to be found."

His father exhales, watching his son, eyes wide.

"And what happened with the... the jaguar or the coyote?" George asked.

"They didn't follow us. I was too scared to try and find the cave again, just grateful to have escaped the first time."

"And Hermano?"

"He found me at the boat. Neither of us said much as we pushed off toward the mainland. Hermano looked worse than I did. We just laid in the boat bleeding and passed out. When I came to, I didn't recognize the shoreline. We'd drifted miles down the coast."

George noticed the slight scar just above his father's eye, a small indention in the skin he'd never seen before.

"Months later, I tried to call him—to hear what he remembered. He picked up... but said he didn't know me. Said we'd never met." His father's eyes dropped. "I can describe the island, but I couldn't find it now if I tried."

For a moment, neither of them spoke. The air in the

room felt charged, like the story had left something behind. A flicker, maybe.

As the quiet set in, his father pulled the comforter across him, Chewbacca roaring into the snowstorm printed across the fabric.

"How am I supposed to sleep after that?" George says. The question goes unanswered.

George watches his father stand, journal closed and tucked under his arm – the leather cover dark and curled at the edges. He turns off the light on the nightstand.

"Dad," George asks, tracing a finger over the bedding, "what about the treasure? If you knew which island, could you find the cave again?"

"I don't know, Jorge," his father pauses, thinking. "Maybe it wasn't meant to be found." Silhouetted, his father pauses, then smiles, just a little. "But who knows."

His father turns away down the hall, and for a moment, everything is quiet.

George rolls onto his side, pulling the blanket up to his chin. The room is still warm with the heat of the jungle, but he feels a chill anyway. His mind drifts to the story, to the cave, to the glyphs no one could read. To the bats.

And to the beasts, who all turn again in his memory and see him lying there. The jaguar's burning eyes. The twisting shadows of the coyote and quetzal.

He tells himself the story will fade by morning. Maybe he'll even forget about the images.

But he knows he won't.

————

CONTINUE READING ON TINYWORLDS.substack.com

ATTRIBUTION

The following song lyrics included which constitute fair use under Section 107 of the Copyright Act of 1976. The song lyrics are the property of their respective owners.

- *Backstage Pass* - Johnny R. Cash
- *Monteagle Mountain* - Richard McGibony
- *What A Fool Believes* - Michael McDonald, Kenny Loggins
- *Spinning Wheel* - David Clayton-Thomas

From *ISLA*:

- Life During Wartime - David Byrne, Chris Frantz, Jerry Harrison, Tina Weymouth
- Spellbound - Siouxsie Sioux (Susan Ballion), John McGeoch, Steven Severin, Budgie
- Are Friends Electric - Gary Numan
- Drug Me - Jello Biafra (Eric Boucher), East Bay Ray, Klaus Flouride, Ted (Bruce Slesinger)
- Achilles Last Stand - Jimmy Page, Robert Plant
- Eclipse - Roger Waters
- Here Comes The Flood - Peter Gabriel

ABOUT THE AUTHOR

J. CURTIS - IS A WRITER WITH A CINEMATIC STORYTELLING STYLE, BLENDING INTRICATE CHARACTERS AND SHARP NARRATIVES. WITH A BACKGROUND IN PRODUCT DESIGN AND FILMMAKING, CURTIS'S WORK DELVES INTO THE QUIET TENSIONS OF MODERN LIFE, CAPTURING FLEETING MOMENTS WHERE THE MUNDANE AND EXTRAORDINARY COLLIDE. HE IS THE AUTHOR OF THE *TINY WORLDS* SHORT FICTION SERIES AND THE FORTHCOMING NOVEL *ISLA*.

Find out more at: jcurtisauthor.com